HIGHLAND FATE

GUARDIANS OF SCOTLAND BOOK 3

VICTORIA ZAK

VICTORIA ZAK ROMANCE

Sign up for Victoria Zak's newsletter on her website to receive a free ebook copy of her
Guardians of Scotland novella
Highland Destiny

You'll also find additional special offers, bonus content and info on new releases.

www.victoriazakromance.com
victoria@victoriazakromance.com

facebook.com/VictoriaZakAuthor

bookbub.com/authors/victoria-zak

instagram.com/victoriazakromance

twitter.com/VictoriaZak2

Highland Fate, Guardians of Scotland Book 3
Victoria Zak
Copyright 2015 by Victoria Zak

Cover Design by JAB Designs

Editing by Kathryn Lynn Davis and Julie Roberts

✻ Created with Vellum

ACKNOWLEDGMENTS

As most of my readers know, this year has been a trying and difficult one. My world came to a screeching halt back in November 2014 when I was diagnosed with breast cancer. I was editing Highland Storm and writing Highland Fate on top of gearing up for the holidays. Needless to say I had to make a lot of decisions that would change my life forever very quickly. When my Oncologist told me, "Victoria, we need to start treatments now." It was clear to me what I had to do, kill my cancer. But I still wanted to write.

I took two months off and then I hit the keys, a slow go but I was writing. Throughout my fight, I could not have made it through my treatments and complete Highland Fate without encouragement from my family, friends, and my readers. You lifted me up when I needed a boost and you gave me the courage to fight. This book is dedicated to all of you who have supported me and those who are still battling this horrible disease.

Victoria Zak

PROLOGUE

*D*eath was but a footstep away. She could hear it, smell it, and feel its outstretched icy fingers clawing at her back. It was only a matter of time before it would hunt her and her daughter down. Like a predator, it displayed unwavering endurance, waiting for the ideal time to attack its quarry. It toyed with her relentlessly day after day, keeping her moving from village to village in order to protect her babe. This was the game from which death derived its greatest pleasure; keeping her on the run.

The sound of blood rushing like a stream through her veins and the heavy thumping of her heart was enough to keep the chase alive. They knew what she possessed would change the world, and they would stop at nothing to gain that control, that power.

A sweet giggle brought the woman's attention to her cherub-cheeked daughter who sat outside, unbalanced, petting a black cat. The cat rubbed against the child's chest and in the blink of an eye, caused the babe to tumble over. Frightened cries exploded from the child's mouth and the furry black feline darted from the scene. Picking up her daughter, the mother dusted the dirt from the wailing child's face and consoled her. "Shhh, there, there, my love. 'Tis only a wee fall. Shhh, ye be well." The mother ever so gently bounced the babe in her arms, knowing her words were far from the truth.

Life would never be well for her as long as she was exposed. She was a sitting target whilst they stayed hidden in the village. It wouldn't be long now before death would pick up their trail, snuff them out and destroy their lives. She could feel it in her bones.

She took the child inside her small thatch-roofed home, and the babe stopped crying once her mother placed her on a blanket with a few small handmade toys to intrigue her curious mind. The babe snatched a wooden doll made out of rowan twigs. She was intrigued by its little white dress. The mother made her way to the bed where she sat and watched her love. Since the day she was born, the child had always been the curious kind, and smart beyond her age. She was no more than six months old and already showed so much promise. Knowing who her father was, there was no doubt that her daughter was different from the average child. If only the babe's father was here now, they would be under his protection.

She blew out a frustrated breath. That dream was far, too far, from reality. The man she'd met over a year ago could never know about his daughter; he could never know her mother's true identity. Her one mistake in leaving her realm had led to a life on the run, but most importantly, it had led her to one amazing man who had given her the most precious gift—a child. But how quickly she had created a mess. Regrets were only for people who felt guilty, and she most definitely did not feel guilty for her actions. She only wished she lived in a world where she could exist freely and happily.

Alas, she could not return to her realm, especially with a child. One look at her and they would know she had broken the rules. One regulation—plainly stated and firmly followed—was that, under no circumstances should anyone leave. It was safe there, unlike the human world where their enemies lurked and waited to steal their magic. Like her daughter she was curious, almost bored. She had left her realm craving a man's touch. Just one night, that's what she'd told herself. One night, then she would return home. But she hadn't planned on meeting the most intriguing man, who in one night loved her thoroughly and made her feel every bit a woman.

And now look where her curiosity had led her; to this strange town, protecting her daughter and staying one step ahead of death. Frankly it was destroying not only her, but ultimately it would also destroy her child.

The babe looked at her mother, yawned, and gave her a smile. A smile with no words, yet it held trust, and she knew what she had to do; she had to keep her daughter safe.

The sun was setting behind the vibrant orange clouds as she opened the door and scanned the outside of her home for death. It was eerily peaceful, too quiet for her liking. Not even the townsfolk stirred. A breeze blew through the village, chilling her to the bone. The time had come again; they had to leave.

As quick as she could, she gathered a few necessities and prepared her horse for travel. Once everything was ready, the mother turned to her babe, who was now fast asleep cuddled with her doll of rowan twigs. The babe slept innocently. Her lips were partly open, her tiny hands fisted and twitching. The mother smiled at her daughter's beauty. As the gray cloud surrounding her darkened, she realized she had to make haste and get them to safety.

Reaching down she took the sleeping bundled babe into her arms and wrapped the child around her chest with a plaid. Tying the last piece of plaid securely around her waist, she slipped outside. Keeping her daughter silent in slumber was imperative. With shaking hands, she grabbed the horse's reins and mounted.

She dug her heels into the animal's sides, indicating the urgency at hand. She had to make it to Dunfermline Abbey. Riding through the night and into mid-morn, she could make it with God's grace. She had to, for evil could not avail there. With one firm squeeze of the woman's legs, the horse shot through the village and disappeared into the forest.

The woman's long brown hair trailed behind her, whipping in the air as she rode through the unforgiving forest. Low-lying tree branches raked at her flawless skin and tore at her flesh. The ground grabbed at the horse's hooves, causing the steed to stumble off balance. But through all her misfortunes, she stood firm; she was determined to make it to safety.

The air chilled and the smell of sulfur grew. Glancing behind her, she could see the forest closing in on her through the glow of the full moon. Tree branches on either side of her began to touch, forming a tunnel. The ground shook as she felt the heaviness of hooves pounding the earth. This couldn't be happening to her. She hadn't spent the last six months in hiding to turn around and be clutched by death's grip. Nay, she would fight it with everything she had.

Abruptly she halted her horse and faced the menace. Black-cloaked figures on horseback appeared at the end of the trail. White foam dripped from the horses' mouths in anticipation of the chase. Death was upon them. She placed her hands in front of her and closed her eyes. Bright white light shot from her hands toward the opening of the tunnel. Trees toppled over, closing the forest between them and their enemies. Harrowing screams of defeat echoed through the woods. They had avoided death this time, but for how long she did not know.

Her babe stirred, wrinkled her forehead, and threatened to fuss. "Shhh, my love. We're almost there." The woman kicked her horse forward and before long the babe fell fast asleep again.

With the threat of danger long since passed, the stone walls of Dunfermline Abbey appeared a hoof beat away, which made the mother slow her pace. It was too soon for their time together to end, but it was the only way to keep her babe safe. Taking in a deep breath, the woman continued on the trail to the gatehouse of the abbey. Gently she dismounted, trying not to disturb the babe. She removed an open basket from the back of her saddle and placed her daughter snugly in it. Taking the basket with shaking hands, she cautiously strode into the gatehouse. No one was there. *Thank the Gods!*

She placed the basket down and kneeled down before it. Her daughter was awake, looking up at her with deep, hazel eyes and outstretched arms. Tears rolled down the woman's cheeks in streams.

Was she really going through with this? Did she actually have the courage to do it, to leave her own flesh and blood? Could she will her legs to walk away from her daughter, abandoning her? The abbey was the safest place for her. The woman was protecting her child, but why did it have to hurt so bad? Her heart was breaking piece by aching piece.

Reaching behind her neck, the mother removed her necklace with an egg-shaped locket dangling at the end of it. She held the locket in both hands and whispered over the trinket, then took the necklace and placed it over the babe's head, hiding the locket underneath her dress. "This will keep ye safe, my love." She kissed her daughter's forehead.

From out of nowhere, a man wearing a long, brown robe ran down the path leading to the gatehouse, calling out to her, "Ye can 'no be in there." The woman looked up in surprise. She had stayed too long. Being caught was not part of her plan. The plan was to leave the babe and walk away. No one was supposed to see her.

Panicked, she ran and quickly mounted her horse, taking off through the forest. When it was safe, she glanced back to make sure the monk had indeed found her daughter. A sobering feeling, yet she smiled, knowing that her babe would be safe now. Death would no longer plague them as long as her daughter stayed at the abbey.

1

*H*eavy footfalls thundered on the ground as Red Hawk strode through the village, infuriated. His broad shoulders twitched and his spine tingled as he immersed himself in thought. He palmed his sgian-dubh, throwing the damn thing up into the air and catching it by its hilt. *How could someone take his generosity for granted?*

The land of Helmfirth thrived with rolling fields of oats, properly equipped with healthy oxen to plow the earth. He'd made sure that the butcher in the village had a never-ending supply of the best meats and poultry and the finest equipment to do his job properly. In fact, Hawk had hunted game himself on several occasions in order to feed his people when times were hard.

There were men-at-arms who defended this land and fought for Hawk with vigor, putting their country before their own lives. And Helmfirth flourished.

In return all Hawk wanted was order in his village. The townsfolk had jobs to do and they did them well or suffered the consequences of disobedience. It was an eye-for-an-eye way of ruling over his people. It became personal when someone stole, cheated, or killed on his land. Not that it happened often, but when it did, he'd show no mercy. He was the Justiciar of Helmfirth, well respected and feared.

There was good reason why Red Hawk led with a tight fist. He didn't trust humans. Nay, he had learned long ago, when a human murdered his father, to keep his enemies close at hand. If it wasn't for his two sisters, he wouldn't give a rat's arse about these people. His sisters needed peace and to live normal human lives. He owed them that.

Undoubtedly the warrior protected this village with his life, making sure Helmfirth thrived for these people and this is how they repaid him? With thievery?

Hawk passed several townsfolk, never once sparing a glance at them. Every last one of them made his gut lurch. The folks knew better than to cross the brooding Highlander's path and scurried out of his way, bowing their heads so as not to meet his eyes.

As he heatedly treaded through the village, Hawk came across an auld woman who was selling fish. Because Helmfirth bordered the sea, it had a busy port for trade and was known for the freshest fish around. He sheathed his sgian-dubh and stopped in front of her. She was no stranger. Once, sometimes twice a day he would buy a bucket of fish from her, before making his way to visit his ferocious friends.

He threw the coins down on the table and snatched a pail. The woman knew better than to make small talk with the warrior today and nodded her head of graying hair, thanking him kindly for his purchase. Hawk humphed and strode off.

Reaching a small stone-fronted building with a thatch roof, he sharply came to a stop before he entered. He slammed the bucket down into the dirt and paced, resolving to calm the rage ripping through his body. This was his sanctuary and he needed to calm his backside down before he entered.

Taking a deep breath in through his nose, his jaw ticked and he exhaled. His dragon stirred relentlessly, begging to be released. His blood pulsed as he tamped down the urge to shift. Looking at the blue skies above him, the Highlander ran his fingers over his short red hair and composed himself, little by little. Once calm, he opened the door and with two strides he entered, bringing the bucket of fish with him.

Dust specks danced in the air as the sun shined through five of the windows lining the opposite wall. Feathers ruffled and talons pranced on perches as the raptors waited in their mews for their food. However, it wasn't entirely the provisions that made the birds of prey excitable; it was their master's presence.

One raptor in particular stood quietly as Hawk approached. The massive goshawk was unhooded and uncaged, perched alone on its jesses, showing remarkable patience as it waited for its master to prepare and tie a leather band around his forearm for the hawk to perch on.

It was illegal to own such prestigious animals, but Hawk cared naught. If caught the punishment was the severing of one's hands. Try as the mighty may, Hawk welcomed a confrontation with the sheriff or even the bloody king himself. If fact, slaying King Robert would right the wrong the king had done to his family years ago. Justice would finally be served.

Hawk worked his jaw back and forth as he tightened the leather strap. "Humans," he spat.

The quaint hut was nestled inside his forest out of sight of the village, and his birds were hidden well. Being the forest dragon he was, and because he spent so much of his time in the glen, he had rescued the five raptors from either starving, being abandoned or whatever other cruelty life had sprung on them. Even though he found great solace around all his birds, nothing came close to the bond he had with his goshawk, Arlen.

A shrill chirp softened his mood for the briefest moment as Hawk approached the raptor and motioned for it to perch on his arm. With ease and trust, the gray-spotted creature accepted and took its claim.

Making his way through the hut, he fed the rest of the birds of prey, marveling at their beauty. He paused and held out a fish to a petite falcon, a merlin. Beautiful and shaking, the female accepted the fish. Gently, Hawk lifted her wing and examined it. "Aye, lass, ye'll fly again." Holding the fish with her talons, the merlin fluffed her wing back against her body while she tore the flesh from the fish. She was the last of the five raptors to heal, and she was a beauty.

Hawk smiled and headed to the door, leaving the feathered beasts to eat.

Outside he looked to the blue crisp sky. It would be a perfect day, if it wasn't for the thief. He shook his head and strode over to a clearing in the glen. Arlen fluffed his feathers and squawked, waiting unwearied to take flight. Once Hawk gave the command the raptor spread its wings. With two pumps of his powerful wings he flew toward the clouds.

Hawk watched the goshawk as it commanded the blue arc and sliced through the clouds. He understood thoroughly how the bird felt in this moment, for he felt the same when he took to the sky, free and dominating.

Taking a seat next to a rowan tree, the warrior watched Arlen fly over the glen. Hawk didn't have as many years behind him as some of the other Dragonkine, nor had he been born dragon. He was of noble birth. His paternal grandmother was the sister of King John, the King of Scotland. His mother Johanna had ties to England; her grandmother had once been married to Edward I, King of England: two lines of royal descent, Gaelic and Norman. Aye, his life wasn't supposed to have turned out like this.

His father had been murdered by the King of Scotland himself, all in the name of the crown. This left his mother fleeing back to England where her heart had always been, leaving behind her three children.

Hawk blew out a frustrated breath as he thought about his mother. He was only a wee lad when she'd abandoned them. There were no goodbyes. As he recalled, the day she left the four of them were walking through the market square, Hawk holding his elder sister's hand and eating an apple while his little sister ran behind them, trying to catch up. From out of nowhere two men approached Johanna. Coin was exchanged and his mother turned and walked away from them, leaving her children with the men. Never looking back, she was gone and he had never seen her again.

The men were cruel as time went by. His sisters had become servants to the rogues, and Hawk was nothing more than a nuisance. Keeping him busy with stable duties kept him out of the stronghold and away from his sisters. Not the noble upbringing they were used to. One of the men, Liam, had quite the thirst for ale. When drunk, which was often, he would seek out Hawk and beat him for something the wee lad didn't understand. Never once had Hawk told his sisters about the abuse, and after a while he became numb to the beatings.

That was until the day Liam had taken it too far and left Hawk unconscious in the stables. Lana, his eldest sister, had found him bloodied and beaten, lying on soiled hay. Even after years passed the only remembrance he had of that night was that at evening meal, strangely, the two men fell asleep after Lana served them their ale. That dreadful night the three of them left the nightmare behind and were suddenly on their own.

Lana cared for Hawk and his younger sister, Gwen, just like a mother. After leaving the slave-house, she worked as a cook for a small clan and in return the abandoned children had a roof over their heads and food in their bellies. Lana had to grow up fast. There was no time to be a child.

When Hawk went through his transformation to Dragonkine, the siblings worked together to help him as he suffered through his muscles being ripped and his bones broken day after day until the change was completed. The girls hid him away from the clan when he was sick. Who knew what they would have thought, seeing such a sick wee lad? Surely they would have been accused of bringing the plague and doom upon the locals.

Indeed, Hawk would sell his soul in order to ensure his sisters' safety and well-being. He owed them that much. Hell, he owed the girls the world. So he took it upon himself to guarantee Lana and Gwen would never suffer again, although how he made that happen was his secret to keep, and the girls never asked how their brother came about owning Helmfirth.

Hawk leaned back against the rowan tree and rested his arms on his propped up knees as he watched his raptor soar down into the loch and catch a fish. Finally he relaxed as he pushed aside his childhood thoughts. He had bigger issues at hand. Someone had stolen from him and the fool had to pay for such a crime.

Leaving his second-in-command, Brodie MacGregor, to deal with the thief had been a tough call, but it had to be done, for Hawk was too angered. And when he was this angry he had a difficult time keeping his dragon stilled. He felt the change overcoming his body. He felt the compulsion to shift.

Lana and Gwen were the only ones who knew his secret and he wanted to keep it that way. Surely some of his men-at-arms had their suspicions, but no one dared to speculate or spread rumors. Hawk kept the village safe, which outweighed any ramblings about a dragon.

If he had his way he would shift into dragon permanently, and live in the glen far away from the townsfolk. Life would be much simpler as a dragon.

Crunching leaves coming from behind him startled Hawk and he jumped to attention, ready to attack.

"Shite, MacGregor, ye must no' sneak up on me like that!"

MacGregor approached with his hands held up in surrender. "My laird." He bowed his head. "I thought ye knew to expect me. The thief has been placed in the pillory and awaits his punishment."

Every bit of pent-up irritation coursed within his veins, pumping rage all over his body. Hawk felt his dragon gain control and his spine stiffen. Ruby-red waves rippled across his eyes. It was time the thief paid.

MacGregor looked to the ground and stood silent while he waited for the Hawk's command.

Cracking his neck from side to side and rolling his massive shoulders back and forth, Hawk made his way back to the village. He held out his right arm and within seconds Arlen landed on his forearm. The bird fluffed his feathers and settled in.

"Och, what did the fool have to say?" Hawk asked as the two men walked toward the village square.

"Nothin'. In fact he hasn't said a word."

"Beg for mercy?" Hawk gave MacGregor a sideways glance.

MacGregor took a double look at Hawk's eyes. They were normal again. "Nay." He paused. "I think the fool may be daft."

Strictly true. Anyone in their right mind would never attempt to steal from the Red Hawk. He cared naught that the stolen property was a stale loaf of bread. Thievery was thievery. Someone had worked hard to bake that bread, had paid for it. And then to cause a ruckus and claim the sweet auld lady had lied and accused the wrong man... Well, that was absurd.

Hawk and MacGregor approached the village with purpose as the last rays of sunlight were settling into dusk. One thing was certain; if this fool made him late to the evening meal he would have the eejit's head. Being late to any meal was inexcusable and furthermore, disrespectful.

As the men strode farther into the town square, a throng of townsfolk gathered around the pillory. The crowd separated as Hawk walked past; MacGregor followed closely behind. Two of his men-at-arms who were standing guard, bowed their heads at Hawk.

"This is the fool?" Hawk eyed the warriors sternly.

"Aye."

He observed the man. His head and his hands were trapped between two pieces of wood, hollowed out so his neck and wrists had little room to move. The man was forced to stand while his head was face down so he could only see the ground. *Pathetic,* Hawk thought.

The Highlander towered over the thief as he perched the goshawk on the pillory. The bird shrieked out loud and pecked the man's ear, causing him to cry out in pain.

"Ye dinnae belong here, do ye?" Hawk crossed his arms over his chest.

"And what makes ye think that?" the thief asked as he wrinkled his face in pain.

As if the goshawk knew that the man was disrespecting his master, he pecked at the man's cheek, breaking the skin.

"One thing ye should know is that I ask the questions. Ye have no rights here!" Hawk's voice, low and deep, carried across the square. The crowd shuddered and mothers grabbed their children close.

Hawk strode toward the back of the pillory. "Everyone here knows ye no' steal from me, unless ye have a death wish."

A sinister laugh slowly escaped the thief.

In one fluid motion Hawk was in front of him. He lifted his knee and bashed the man in the mouth. "Ye mock me? Are ye senseless?"

The thief spat blood and tried to lift his head. "Och, ye see, ye all be already dead."

Hawk grabbed a handful of the man's hair and yanked it back until the wood dug into his neck. "What do ye mean, we are all dead?"

The thief struggled to talk. "Why...should I tell ye? All I wanted was to fill me belly."

Thievery was now the last thing on Hawk's mind. How was he supposed to protect his sisters and his village if he didn't know what this fool was conjuring?

"Thief," Hawk lowered his head to ear level so the fool could hear him loud and well, "I know ye be a stranger and ye dinnae belong here, which leads me to believe ye came with ill intentions. Ye can make this easier on yerself and tell me what's coming, or I can beat it out of ye."

The man gave Hawk a twisted smile. At this point Hawk was left with no other choice. One way or another he would get the information he wanted. He nodded and the goshawk charged the man's head, pecking out his eye. The thief screamed out in agonizing pain.

"Are ye ready to talk?" Hawk asked. "Or shall Arlen take yer other eye?"

"Aye!" The man was breathless. "Please!"

For Hawk, patience had never been a virtue and this fool had pushed him to the limit. "Go on then."

Blood dripped from the stranger's right eye and his voice shook. "Ships will be entering the harbor in less than a day's time."

"Ships? And who is advancing this attack on Helmfirth?" As peaceful as Hawk tried to be, there was always someone out there craving what was his. Or someone wanting to challenge him. But who? Helmfirth was secluded, with not a neighboring clan around for at least a three-day ride.

"It's no' who, my laird, it's death."

"How am I supposed to trust ye?" Hawk demanded.

"Och my laird, that's a risk ye must be willing to take."

"Bastard!" Hawk shoved the man's head away and paced in front of the pillory. What was he going to do? *I can no' trust this eejit. But what if he's right and Helmfirth is in danger?* If he could spew his venomous poison right now and melt the skin from this fool's body, he would do it quicker than he could shift.

MacGregor came up behind him and stood shoulder to shoulder. "My laird, I can lead half of our men to the harbor while the other half stay here to protect the village."

Always prepared and ready for battle, it was like MacGregor to have a plan. It was one of the reasons Hawk trusted him and had allowed him to wed Lana. He was an honorable man who provided for his family and fought for Helmfirth.

"Nay, send full force. I'll stay here tonight and meet ye on the morrow."

"Aye." MacGregor strode toward the stables, motioning his men to follow suit.

Hawk sent the thief a vile stare as he quit the square, calling over his shoulder to one of the guards, "And chain this thief in the dungeon. I'm no' done with him yet."

Without hesitation two of his men busied themselves obeying their laird's command.

No doubt one dragon, especially with his size and deadly venom, could protect Helmfirth if the threat showed true. He wasn't scared of death; in fact he welcomed it, dared it. There was a reason his stronghold had held throughout the years: magic. No amount of weapons or strategic war tactics could penetrate the power of magic. As long as he lived, which was forever, this village would be protected. His sisters would be safe, but he had to keep his head.

~

*H*awk's belly rumbled as soon as he opened the doors to the great hall. The aroma of cooked fish, vegetables, and bread made his mouth water. The cooks had done a fine job this eve. The hall at Helmfirth was only half filled as the Red Hawk's warriors prepared for battle and their journey to the harbor. Still the thief had left him unsettled, which irritated him. All he wanted to do was enjoy his meal with a peaceful mind.

Hawk sat his big body down at a table in front of a trencher and started to pile the night's provisions high. The scowl on his face was more than a warning that he wanted to be left alone.

"Ye dinnae have to be a grump all the time," Lana said as she sat across from her brother and filled a tankard with mead.

Hawk glanced up, chewing a mouthful of bread. "Lana." He swallowed. "I do no' need yer teasing."

Lana handed the tankard to him. "I know, but if ye smile once in a while, ye might grab the attention of a lass. Ye have a handsome smile, Hawk."

"I need no lass. Ye and yer sister keep me busy enough." He took a long pull from the tankard. "Just the other day I had to get rid of a lad pursuing Gwen's womanly virtues."

"Och, brother, please tell me it wasn't the Drummond lad," Lana said disappointedly.

"Aye! I picked the lad up by the seat of his trews and kicked his arse oot. That one is no good, Lana. Trust me, I know."

Gwen's beauty caught the attention of many lads. Keeping that lass's virginity intact until she wed was going to be the death of him.

Lana shook her head and filled her trencher. "I guess that makes me lucky. Ye liked MacGregor." She smiled as her husband's name passed her lips.

Hawk looked at his sister and grumbled, shoving a piece of fish in his mouth.

At that moment MacGregor appeared in the great hall, making his way to his wife as he balanced one of his sons on his shoulders and one wrapped around his leg while the eldest lad walked proudly beside him. "There be me bonny wife." He bent down and kissed Lana on the cheek.

"Good eve, husband. Are ye hungry?" Before MacGregor could answer, the three mischievous lads called out in unison, "Meeee!" Lana giggled and grabbed three trenchers, filling them with food.

Hawk peered up to watch the chaotic feeding frenzy and smirked. Lana was happy and had a loving family, a family she deserved. Then he looked at MacGregor, who had caught him smiling. MacGregor smiled back. "Ye know life is worth living when the right lass comes along."

Hawk's moment of good spirits turned serious and tiresome. Why the sudden interest in his love affairs? It was not that he didn't enjoy a lass; he had never tried it.

Settling down, taking a wife was not a topic he visited much. This was a touchy subject for most Dragonkine, though deep down he had thought about how it would feel to be loved by a lass. He had dared to think about waking up in the morn next to a soft warm female body. But Hawk was smart; he protected his heart and would never allow himself to chase that dream. It would only bring him heartache and despair and, frankly, he'd had enough of that in his life. An immortal dragon life did have its downfalls.

The warrior stiffened his spine and acted as if he hadn't heard MacGregor's comment. "Are your men ready for travel?"

"Aye. I wanted to kiss me wife farewell before I left. We'll ride through the night and arrive at the harbor before sunrise."

"Good." Hawk drank from his tankard of ale.

"My laird, are ye sure ye want all of our men at the port? We can spare a few to stay behind."

"Do ye query me command?" Hawk peered at him sternly.

"Nay, my laird."

"Good. Now if ye will excuse me, I'm going to me bedchamber." He took a loaf of bread with him as he stood, but before he left the great hall he said his farewells to Lana and kissed her boys on the top of their heads.

"Uncle Hawk," the eldest boy called out. "When can ye and da take me huntin'?"

"Och, I dinnae..."

"I've been practicing wit' me bow real good. Haven't I Da?" The boy gleamed at his father excitedly.

MacGregor smiled proudly. "Aye, ye have, but yer uncle is a verra busy man. When I return I'll take ye huntin'."

The boy's look of disappointment crushed Hawk like a boulder slamming into him. He never allowed himself to get close to the boys, or MacGregor, as a matter of fact. It was easier on him to stay away and be alone. It had taken a long time to build up these walls; he wasn't going to let them be breached by anyone.

Hawk could no longer look at his nephew without feeling like an arse, so he strode off to his bedchamber, once again alone.

2

*H*awk's massive naked body filled his bed as he lay on his back wide-awake, restless. *Death is coming.* The thief's warning plagued him, causing a wave of questions to crash down on him one after another. What did it mean, 'death is coming'? Moreover, how was he going to stop it? His plan so far was to shift. Aye, his secret would be out, but not knowing what was threatening Helmfirth, he had no other choice. A dragon could escape death. With his venomous poison, he could fight off any army at full force. Hell, make that two armies at once; the more humans dead the better.

The impulse to shift made his skin itch and he began to sweat. His blood raced as if seeking out a desirable destination. His pulse thumped so loud that he could feel it in his ears. Quickly, Hawk sat up and cursed, "God's Blood!" Running his hand through his red hair, he hopped to his feet and briskly walked to the water basin. He splashed the cold water over his face and shoulders and when that didn't calm him, he dumped the whole basin over his head.

Death is coming, looped around his thoughts. Hawk couldn't shake the uneasiness, or the eerie feeling the thief had left gnawing at his gut. Wrapping his plaid around his waist, he grabbed a tunic and boots and headed to the dungeon. There was only one way to obtain the answers he sought, and that was by force.

Dawn cracked through the mist-covered sky that hovered over the stillness of the village as Hawk stepped outside and made his way to the dungeon. There were two entrances; one inside the keep next to the kitchen and one outside, hidden among the stone and mortar. Forever walking that delicate line between shifting and remaining in his human body, Hawk preferred the hidden way to the dungeon. It gave him time to clear his thoughts and tamp down the beast inside.

Once at the top of the dark, narrow stairway, he took the steps two at a time, snatching a fiery torch along the way. Taking in a deep breath, he continued down a cramped corridor, scraping his shoulders on the rough stone walls. God's Blood, he hated it down here. One thing was certain, confined spaces made a dragon's skin crawl.

At the end of the corridor the room opened up to one cell. There were no bars, just an open area in which a thief confined to a pillory stood taking up the space. The prisoner lifted his head as far as the wood behind his neck would let him. He smirked. "My laird."

Hawk placed the torch on a nearby stand. The flames flickered throughout the room like lightning. The warrior was now facing the thief as he crossed his arms over his chest. His stance said truly that he was not to be taken lightly. "I didnae come here for small talk. I want to know who's planning the attack."

"I told ye, death."

Before the prisoner saw it coming, Hawk slammed his right fist against the man's jaw. Blood poured from his mouth as he spat out a tooth.

The warrior stood back, regaining his self-control. He was always in control. "I asked ye a question and ye will answer it."

The thief cracked his neck and fisted his hands until his knuckles turned white. His back, once hunched over, became elongated, popping vertebra by vertebra. The wood from the pillory cracked and splintered as his thicken.

Stunned, Hawk took another step back. Was the thief shifting? He could not be a dragon; Hawk would have known. Not trusting his own eyes, Hawk blinked at the sight before him.

Splintered wood scattered about the room as the thief smashed through his restraints. His lips peeled back, revealing long fangs. Opening his arms to the ceiling, he threw back his head and bellowed.

Grabbing his dirk, Hawk stood ready to fight until he saw the man grow another head. "God's Blood! What are ye?"

One of the wyvern's heads snaked forward, snapping its dagger-sharp teeth, just missing tearing a hunk of flesh from Hawk's chest. With stealth-like reflexes that only a true Dragonkine warrior possessed, Hawk stabbed the gnarly, salivating head with his dirk, sending the creature shrieking.

Heedfully, Hawk walked over to the second head and surprisingly, it was quiet. There was no movement, and it looked as if it was sorrowful with regret. As Hawk came in sight of the wyvern it turned and looked at him.

"What are ye?" Hawk asked.

"It does no' matter. If ye want to live and save Helmfirth, kill me now." The wyvern hung its head stretching out its neck, waiting for the fatal blow.

Not only did this creature make his skin crawl, but now it was irritating him. "Are ye the threat?"

"We were sent here to—"

At that moment the dominant head swung around, knocking Hawk off his feet. His head slammed down onto the stone floor; his vision blurred.

"Ye backbiting bastard! Ye were going to tell our enemy the plan!" The vile winged creature shouted at its submissive part, who stood quiet. "We were sent here to do a job and I'll see it done." The wyvern advanced on Hawk.

Blinking rapidly, Hawk fought to regain his vision. He slashed out with his dagger, hoping to connect with the creature, but alas, he sliced through thin air, connecting to nothing. An odious laugh echoed through the cell, mocking his distress, as if the creature knew

Hawk couldn't best him. The wyvern charged the warrior. Hawk couldn't move quickly enough and the wyvern snatched him up in its mouth and bit the side of his abdomen. Dagger teeth sank into his skin, ripping his flesh from his body. With strength like the Gods, the two-headed beast threw Hawk across the dungeon.

Hawk landed near the stairwell, cracking his head on the stone steps. How was he going to kill this beast? Pain shot through his head and blood poured from the right side of his stomach. As Hawk looked around the dungeon searching for the wyvern, he called forth his dragon. Dragon heat surged within him as he anticipated the shift. Finding it odd that the wyvern had halted the attack, he was still on high alert, when black smoke began to swirl throughout the room.

The smoke wafted over Hawk, causing him to feel dizzy. A sense of panic took over when he could no longer feel his dragon, nor the shift. Pain shot through his stomach and he doubled over. "What's happening to me?" he moaned.

A loud shriek bit through the thickening smoke. Plagued by weakness, Hawk slowly lifted his head toward the high-pitched noise. Stunned, he couldn't believe his eyes; the two-headed wyvern stood in the middle of a cloud of smoke, shrouded in blackness with its wings stretched out to the sky as if calling forth the horrid haze.

The sludge in the air settled in Hawk's lungs, making it hard to breathe. If he was going to make it out of here alive, he had to shift. There was no other way. He had to give his dragon one more chance. With Every bit of effort he had left, he closed his eyes and reached down deep for his dragon. It wouldn't be long now. His dragon never failed him.

With much distress, Hawk couldn't understand why his dragon was refusing the shift. He reached farther, dug deeper, but the dragon was nowhere to be found. It was as if his dragon was gone. He felt nothing and he was growing weaker by the second.

"Run, ye fool! It's a trap! Run NOW!" the submissive part of the wyvern warned.

Hawk could hear someone warn him, but his bloody body wouldn't move. For the first time in his dragon years, he was scared.

The one and only thing he trusted and counted on had failed him. What was happening to him? He had been drugged by the smoke... bedeviled. Reality set in and his will to survive took over. Using all his strength, he struggled to his hands and knees and crawled toward the stairs.

~

*H*elmfirth's harbor was no more than a night's ride through the glen, following the loch to the river. Locals fished the river for salmon which was one of Helmfirth's most prized exports. Men also built boats there to transport their goods to neighboring clans. If the harbor were to be sieged, it would be economically devastating to Helmfirth.

Riding throughout the night, MacGregor and his men made it to the harbor in record time. With haste, the well-trained and obedient warriors took their places at their posts and cleared the harbor of all activity. MacGregor, on horseback, rode to each one of his men, making sure his soldiers were ready for battle. Not knowing what they were up against, everyone was on full alert.

Dawn broke and on into the long midday hours there was no movement along the harbor. Furthermore there was no sign of the Red Hawk, which left a bad feeling stirring within MacGregor. Something was awry; it gnawed at his gut relentlessly.

At MacGregor's vantage point he could see up the river to the harbor. All morning waiting for the attack had been testing his patience. And unaware where his laird was...well, MacGregor couldn't think about that now. He had a job to do; secure the harbor. "Sir." One of his men strode up to him. "There's been no movement."

"Aye. Something seems amiss here." With a keen eye, MacGregor patrolled the river. *Where are the bastards?*

From out of nowhere, three longboats sailed downstream toward the harbor's dock. The men held true in their battle stance, waiting for their commander's orders. MacGregor motioned for his men to hold tight, to not make a move.

As the longboats came closer to the dock the tension could be felt miles away. Horses pranced, waiting to charge, and warriors palmed their swords in anticipation of a bloody battle. Eager faces twitched, jaws clenched tight, and teeth ground together. Thus far the warriors were battle bound and ready to fight.

Once MacGregor had a clear view, he noticed there was no one on the boats. "Bloody Hell!" Hastily MacGregor rode over to a group of his men. "Taran, lead your men to the dock and search the boats."

"Aye."

Distraught, MacGregor paced the tree line overlooking the dock. *How could this be?* Was this some form of trickery to draw the warriors away from Helmfirth and leave his laird and village unprotected, and furthermore, his wife and children?

Time stood still as the warrior waited to hear from Taran. "This could no' be." A bone-chilling thought slammed into MacGregor and he froze. Ghost ships. Missing laird. "Holy Hell!" This was a diversion. The real attack was happening right now in Helmfirth. "It's a diversion!" he called out. "To the keep!" And as if his arse had gone up in flames, MacGregor and his men rode hard back to Helmfirth, praying that they weren't too late.

3

*C*rawling up the stairs to the dungeon door, Hawk stood on weak, shaking legs. With all his strength, he threw his body into the door, cracking it. As the door opened he tumbled to the ground, causing the local townsfolk walking by to scatter. But it wasn't the sight of their wounded laird that made them run; it was the two-headed, salivating devil behind him that had the people running for their lives.

Hawk, on his back, tried to crawl out of the way of the wyvern's massive foot as it kicked him. The powerful blow flung Hawk through the air, launching him onto the roof of the butcher's shop. His body fell through the splintering wood and crashed to the ground in a heap. Debris rained down onto his body, as he lay unable to move.

The wyvern screeched with delight as he sent blood-chilling fear throughout the village. People frantically bounced off one another as they scattered, desperate to find a place to hide. Unfortunately, there was nowhere to hide as the creature blasted the village with flames. Townsfolk on fire ran, some melted right in front of the few lucky ones who had avoided the heat blast.

When Hawk came to, his first thoughts were of his sisters. Where were they? He had to get them to the keep. They would be safe there as the keep was cloaked with magic. But the problem was he had been weakened and could no longer feel his dragon. He was defenseless and frankly this bastard of a monster had pushed him over the edge. Fury like never before raged through him as he found the strength to brush off the shattered wood and stand. "Och, ye bloody bastard. Yer fight is with me. I suggest ye finish what ye started. I'm no' dead!" Hawk picked up a long piece of wood and with the sharp end he approached the foul beast.

From out of the glen Helmfirth men, led by MacGregor, roared their war cry and charged the village, abruptly stopping when the wyvern came into view. The warhorses neighed nervously and fought their riders, attempting to flee the scene when the beast snarled and snapped its fangs at them.

"MacGregor?" Hawk was surprised and quite honestly relieved to see his second-in-command with, as always, impeccable timing. "Find my sisters and take them to the keep!"

But before MacGregor could will his legs to move, right before his eyes, the wyvern spun around and grabbed Hawk by his midsection with its mouth. With the odds greatly in his favor, the creature picked the Highlander up and threw him forcefully to the ground.

The rest of MacGregor's men charged the beast with every possible weapon they could find. Long spears jabbed at the beast's flesh, only to be broken from the toughness of its skin. Arrows were aimed and shot at its head; alas this gesture merely irritated the wyvern, feeling like pesky flies to him rather than managing to wound him. But nonetheless the men were determined to bring the monster down and save their home.

As the men battled the beast, time moved in slow motion while MacGregor ran to his laird. "Nay!" Hawk laid on the ground unconscious, bloodied, and broken. Bending down on his knees, MacGregor picked Hawk's head up and noticed that he was breathing; barely, but he was breathing. In all their time together MacGregor had never seen his commander, his brother, so defenseless—helpless. He had to get Hawk out of there. If he stayed any longer, that horrendous two-headed devil would surely be the death of his laird.

"Hawk, can ye hear me? I'm going to get ye oot of here." MacGregor whistled for his horse. A black as night stallion appeared as MacGregor pulled Hawk to his feet. Another Helmfirth warrior ran to his aid and helped MacGregor steady the Red Hawk. The Highlanders hoisted the large man on top of the horse as best as they could. "God speed, my friend," MacGregor whispered into the black steed's ear and with a swift smack on the hindquarters, the warhorse charged through the village toward the forest, away from the bloody scene.

Now it was time for MacGregor to find his wife and children. But first he needed, nay craved, to kill the beast that threatened his home. Drawing his sword high and over his shoulder, MacGregor advanced on the wyvern, slicing at its wings. With one swoop of its wings, it knocked him off his feet and onto his back. "Bloody Hell!"

A bloodcurdling screech unlike anything he had ever heard echoed from above. At first, MacGregor swore it came from the two-headed monster; but nay, the sound most definitely came from above. He dared to glance up at the sky and take his eyes off the enemy. A huge, green winged creature came into view and circled above as if he was getting ready to land in the village. "Nay," he whispered. "It can no' be. A dragon?"

The dust parted as the dragon landed with a powerful thud. The effect made the ground ripple. Back stepping from the dragon, the wyvern halted its attack as if it was taken aback by the mere existence of the beast.

Before the enemy could call forth his black magic, the dragon charged the wyvern head first, impaling one of its three massive horns in the creature's gut. The creature shrieked in pain and ran away. Fortunately, the dragon was not far behind and chased the wyvern into the glen far away from the village.

"MacGregor!" Lana cried out and ran to her husband. "Are ye alright?"

Dumbfounded to what he had witnessed, MacGregor jumped to his feet and grabbed his wife's arm. "Get to the keep, now!"

4

*D*unfermline Abbey

*E*xcited beyond compare, Sister Kate rushed upstairs to the nun's dormitory. Once inside her chamber, she tossed her cloak on a small cot of a bed and slipped out of her long black tunic dress. Like the day before, a fresh bowl of water waited for her to wash up for the day. Without haste, she splashed the cool water on her face. Her day had started like every other day in the abbey with the prayer bells ringing in the dead of the early morn. Three services had already passed and still the sun slept, but not Sister Kate.

After drying her face, she carefully removed her black veil. As it was, there weren't too many clothing choices to decide on. From the moment Kate had taken her vows to become a nun she had been subjected to the rules of the abbey, which governed every aspect of her life, from how she spent her days to how she spent her nights alone with her own thoughts; these were considered the devil's hours.

Abandoned here by her mother as a wee babe, she had only ever known abbey life, so the vows were simple to Kate. She could no longer own property, never marry, and she had to obey the orders of Abbot Benard, who sent his orders through Abbess Margaret.

The nunnery was small and secretive with thirteen sisters, including the Abbess. The sisters had been good to her growing up, all but Abbess Margaret. The Abbess made sure the sisters obeyed the rules and even when they did, it was never good enough for her. In time Kate learned how to deal with the Abbess's temper and only needed to be reminded once that rules were to be obeyed. She could still hear Margaret's authoritative lecture: "Hair short, dress black, veil covers forehead. Stay on the covered path, for the path is the way to God, study religious text, and earn your keep. But above all, always show obedience."

Kate ran her wet fingers through her short brown hair, stopping below her earlobes where the strands ended. Aye, abbey life was difficult at times, but this was home and she was safe here. But that did not mean she wasn't sometimes restless. Giving herself a quick mental shake, Kate slipped on a clean black tunic dress and veil. Time was passing her by. Since this was the only time during her busy day for self-reflection, she needed to pick up the pace. Walking over to the cot, she flung her cloak over her shoulders, grabbed her journal and headed for the door.

Outside Kate walked the cloister. The sun was peeking through the misty clouds, yet the torches still lit the covered pathway. Digging in the pocket of her cloak, she retrieved the note she had been overjoyed and excited about. She fumbled with the parchment, itching to open it. It wasn't every day that she heard from her best friend Abigale Bruce.

The last note she'd read from Abigale had come over a month ago. Kate knew her friend had married James Douglas, at first to Abigale's dismay; but now she was happy and expecting a babe. There were many times, especially when Abigale had lived at the abbey, that Kate had wondered what it would be like to be a princess, to have long hair, to be able to marry, and to have a will of one's own. Abigale never took the vows to become a nun; she had her own fate, a path Kate could never walk. It was wrong to envy her friend, yet she couldn't help it; she had a curious mind.

A turn to the right and down another covered pathway and she reached the garden. It was absolutely stunning this time of year. The days were warm, and she could feel the sunshine lightly kissing her skin, but the nights were cold. It was the perfect time of the year, when the herbs and flowers bloomed. Kate could smell their fragrant scents throughout the abbey. The garden was Kate's favorite place to escape. There was no room here for study, because the sights were too beautiful to pass by. Keeping her nose buried in a book felt like more of a sin than not.

Kate bent down on her knees to examine the garden's array of colorful purple, pink, and yellow flowers. "The butterflies will be coming soon," she said. Picking a bright yellow buttercup, she admired it for a while. Oh how she wished she could stick the velvety cluster of petals in her hair and feel beautiful, but unfortunately that would be breaking the rules.

Blowing out a frustrated breath, she opened her journal and placed the wee flower between two pages then closed it, as she often did. She would dry the flowers between the pages of her journal and then write down information or mayhap draw a few pictures of the blossom. It was especially exciting when the butterflies visited, or even an out-of-the-ordinary insect. She desired to explore more of Mother Nature's beauty, and someday she would, even if she had to beg and plead with Abbot Benard to take her with him into town on business. Although gaining the courage to ask would be a task in itself.

Morning birds sang and chirped as Kate settled herself on a bench. She closed her eyes and took in a deep breath. Indeed this was her escape from abbey life. Realizing she still had Abigale's note in her hand, she opened her eyes and unrolled the parchment. Kate couldn't wait to read it and find out if Abigale had had the babe, but most importantly, how she had fared giving birth. Immediately she immersed herself in her friend's world.

*D*earest Kate,

    I pray that this letter finds ye well. I miss ye dearly and wish I could visit. A fortnight ago I gave birth to a beautiful daughter. We named her Jamie and she looks just like her father, even her eyes. The birth was challenging, but I fared well. James worried me some. I truly felt like he wanted a boy and was disappointed in me, but that was far from the truth. Oh Kate, I wish ye were here. I promise to come visit soon.

    Abigale

*T*ears pooled in the corner of Kate's hazel eyes. Truly she was happy for her friend. She had found love, not only with a man but with a child. Such a precious gift from God and He had blessed Abigale with a wee baby girl. Kate's tears turned to sobs as she thought about her mother. Really there was nothing to remember her by, except for the egg-shaped amulet Kate wore around her neck. She never took it off, and hid it underneath her dress. She felt as one with her mother as the necklace hung right next to her heart, even though she would never know the reason why the woman had left her here at such a young age. After years of asking Abbess Margaret questions, she was no closer to the truth. Of course, Kate had her own opinion about her mother; at first she was hurt when she grasped there would be no visits from her parents; she was alone. Anger festered deep inside until one day she decided to forgive her mother and move on. But the wounds still hurt even to this day.

Wiping her eyes with the back of her hand, she sniffed back the tears and gathered her belongings. Time was passing by fast and she needed to prepare for work. There was no point in bringing up an unsavory past she had long since laid to rest.

Suddenly a noise came from outside the abbey walls, reminding Kate that she was not alone. Alarmed, she stood and held her journal to her chest as if the book of bound pages could shield her from harm. The mysterious sound echoed across the abbey and Kate's heart quickened as she intently listened to the heavy hooves beating across the ground then coming to an abrupt stop. What kind of creature was out there?

She had heard stories from the mason workers about the creatures that lurked in the nearby forest. They had said a winged monster lived in those woods and gorged on human bones. One worker had said he'd seen it with his very own eyes. As he told the tale, he drank his ale and slurred his words. Never really believing in the unnatural, Kate had shrugged off the stories, until now.

Deep, skin-chilling breaths came from the creature as it restlessly pawed at the earth. It sounded so close. In a second Kate was ready to run. If there was a creature out there, she wasn't staying to see what it was, or allowing her bones to be feasted upon. Then she heard a distinctive neigh. Relieved and feeling utterly daft, she exhaled. "A horse." She smiled. Shaking her head, Kate dismissed the lurking, bone-eating creature.

For the sake of her sanity, she walked down the stone path back to the nun's dormitory, until a moan froze her where she stood. The moan came again, sounding more distraught. Kate turned in the direction the sound was coming from. *That was no' a horse's moan.* Looking across the green rolling hill dotted with sheep, she saw the wall was still a distance away. Surely Brother Tom at the gatehouse could take care of this disturbance. The abbey walls were built to keep spiritual life inside and the worldly temptations outside. She would be safe. *Just stay on the path, Kate.*

Again she heard the cry for help; someone was in pain. She took a step closer to the edge of the path. She had never strayed from the cloister; like the walls, there were boundaries and they were not to be crossed. "Stay on the path and it will lead you to God," Kate reminded herself, and turned to continue her path to the dormitory. Another moan so pitiful it shook her soul; she couldn't shake the feeling that she had to help whoever was out there. Temptation was always one step away.

The next time she heard the groan, Kate dropped her journal, lifted her dress, and took off across the field as if her body was not her own to control. Sheep bleated and darted out of her way. Her heart pounded against her ribcage. She wasn't sure if it was because of her Godspeed or from the pure excitement of it all; she did not care. Someone needed help.

With the gatehouse fast approaching, Kate noticed Brother Tom was nowhere to be found. *Where is he?* She slowed her pace once inside, whirling around, frantically searching for the monk. "Brother Tom!" she called out. No one replied. Then she realized...she was standing under the archway of the gatehouse—one step away from the outside world.

Then she saw it, and couldn't believe; her eyes widened. A man, big and full of brawn, lay hunched over a black horse's neck. The fine steed shook its head up and down as though trying to communicate. As she stood staring at the man, blood seeped through his tunic from wounds up and down his back. He needed her help.

Tearing her eyes away from him, Kate gazed down at the threshold, the line that divided her world—the end of the abbey's boundaries and the beginning of the unknown. For Kate this was more than just a threshold; it was time she made a decision. Stay on the path, go and get help or break her rules and help this man in need. Temptation was always one step away.

One footstep into the outside world and all was forgotten except for the wounded man. Kate cautiously addressed him as she neared the horse. "Sir...sir, are ye well?" The man groaned. This man was like nothing she had ever seen before; the mere size of him was intimidating. She gave pause and swallowed hard. *This man needs me help.* Vigilantly, she reached out and touched his thigh, shaking him, trying to make him come to. "Sir!" This time she said it a little louder. The man did not answer and slipped off the horse, falling to the ground.

"Oh, Mother Mary!" Kate dropped to her knees. Her eyes wide and her hands shaking, she ripped the man's tunic free from his body. Deep cuts slashed his torso and blood smeared his skin. She didn't know where to start, nor did she know what to do. If Abigale was here, with her healing abilities, mayhap the man would have a chance.

At that moment Brother Tom came running from the gatehouse in panic. "Sister Kate!" he said breathlessly. "What has happened?"

Kate sat back on her heels in shock, gaping. She couldn't speak. She couldn't move. All she could do was sit and stare at the wounds and shake her head from side to side.

Brother Tom quickly looked the injured man up and down. "We need to get him to the infirmary." The monk pulled the man up by his arms, then looked at Kate still sitting on the ground. "Sister Kate! This man needs yer help."

Kate nodded and stood. "Aye."

With the monk and Kate on either side of the wounded man, they struggled their way to the infirmary. Kate silently prayed over the Highlander that they would reach help before he met his death.

$\mathcal{K}$ate's plan was to help Brother Tom to the infirmary and then leave, but her heart won an inner battle and she stayed. Why she couldn't will herself to go on about her business was beyond her understanding. Something pulled deep within her, causing her to throw caution to the wind. If she believed in magic, she would have thought she had been bewitched by some spell. Her body now had a mind of its own, discarding all good sense.

It wasn't as if there was free time in her busy schedule to be pacing the infirmary and feeling lightheaded from the sight of blood. Two prayer bells had passed and she was late with her daily assessments. Abbess Margaret would not be pleased. Kate would be held responsible for these actions, for not obeying.

"Sister Kate, I need you to hold pressure on this wound," the monk barked out his orders.

Kate froze in mid-pace. Being in there made her stomach flop like a fish out of water from the smell and sight of blood. When Abigale had been at the abbey, Kate rarely had to set foot in this place. Her friend knew that she paled every time she entered, so Abigale took mercy on her and reported back to her about which supplies were needed, allowing Kate to stay away from the infirmary.

Why hadn't she left when she'd had the chance? Hesitantly Kate walked to the bed where the large, unconscious man lay. The monk quickly grabbed her hand and placed it on a chest wound. Blood soaked through the red hair, through the white linen cloth and onto her hands. Sweat beaded across her forehead at the sight and her knees threatened to buckle. *Focus, Kate, focus.*

Swallowing back the bile that collected in the back of her throat, she dared a glance at the Highlander. Brown freckles dotted his broad chest up to his thick neck. His masculine jawline was covered in red, bristly hair. Kate reached out and touched his jaw, caressing his cheek with a trembling hand. By the saints, this man was like nothing she had ever seen. Not that she had much experience with men, but she knew enough. Not even the masons who worked with heavy stone had a physique like this Highlander.

Her heart hastened as he piqued her curiosity even more. She continued farther down his thick neck, where she noticed how large his veins were. The flopping fish in her stomach settled and was replaced by something she had never experienced before. Places that she couldn't imagine started to tingle throughout her body. Aye, this was a spell, the devil's work. From out of nowhere this man had appeared and bewitched her without saying a word. It had to be a test from God, a test to keep her on the spiritual path, and she was failing miserably.

Cold blood seeped across her hand, reminding her that the patient was seriously injured. Removing the cloth, she paused in horror. Through all the blood that pooled to the surface, she could see this was no battle wound. Large teeth marks marred the skin as if an animal had ripped his flesh from his body. Staring at the large, jagged wound, she wondered what kind of animal could have left behind such a horrific injury. Whatever it was, it had to have been bigger than any animal in the glen. Not even a bear had a mouth that big.

Breaking her thoughts, the monk pushed her aside to tend to his patient. "Yer work here is done, ye may leave now."

Taking a step back, Kate shook her head, struggling to erase what she had witnessed, for if there was a beastie out there with the ability to best a Highlander the size of this man—well, quite frankly she didn't want to think about it. Mayhap the drunken mason was right after all.

Before she left, Kate took one last glance at the Highlander and prayed for the monk to save him. Something deep inside told her the man needed more than faith; he needed a miracle. Quickly she left his bedside and strode to the wash bowl, scrubbing her bloodstained hands, then readied herself for the wrath of Abbess Margaret.

ate begged the abbess for forgiveness for her disobedient behavior. She explained that a wounded man had arrived at the abbey in desperate need of help and that the monk in the infirmary had asked for her assistance. The abbess stood with her arms crossed over her chest in disapproval. "Tis' no' yer duty to be assisting in the infirmary." Disappointment dripped from every word.

Knowing better than to speak, Kate stood, shoulders slumped, and her gaze fixated on the ground.

The abbess ordered her to her room to pray for her sins.

Kate nodded and made her way back to the dormitory, keeping her eyes down and staying on the path.

Shutting the door behind her, she closed her eyes and rested her back against the door. Taking in a deep breath, she knew what she had to do. It was the only way to purify the body, mind and soul, to make her accountable for disobeying. She had been weak, tempted by the devil.

Pushing herself off the door, Kate untied her cloak and laid it on the bed. She proceeded to undress. She laid the black tunic next to her cloak, then unpinned her veil and laid that next to the dress. Now that she was completely naked except for the necklace she never removed, she was ready to cleanse her body, but most importantly, to cleanse her soul.

With determination Kate walked to her bedside dresser, bent down, and slid her hand underneath, looking for a small key. She picked it up and quickly unlocked the only drawer in her nightstand. One click, then another and the drawer opened. Swallowing hard, Kate lightly touched a black handle wrapped in leather, following the wrapping to the end. She ever so gently lifted one of the multiple strips of leather and held it in her hand. It had been a while since she'd used this device; if only she had stayed on the path.

Picking up the leather whip, she stood and straightened her spine. There was no doubt she had to be punished. She took it in her right hand and crossed it over her left shoulder, sending the slender straps across her back. The straps were long and stopped right before her buttocks. Her body jerked with the initial slap. She hissed in pain. Indeed it had been a long time since she had felt the sting of the leather. Keeping her attention on her task, she slowly slid the straps up her back, then took the whip in her left hand and repeated the motion on the right side of her back. This time her body accepted the pain and she didn't flinch. Tears slid down her cheeks, not from the bitter sting, but from being ashamed of her actions.

Sweat mixed with blood glistened on her exhausted body as Kate repeated this process four times. Laying the whip back in the drawer, she locked it away. Her legs shook from the pain as she made her way to the bed before her body succumbed to the ache, and before long she fell into a light sleep before she'd had the chance to clean her wounds. In fact Kate didn't think she could handle that kind of pain yet. She needed rest.

She drifted in and out of sleep, her thoughts on the red-headed man in the infirmary. It wasn't every day that a man of this stature came to the abbey and, frankly, it disturbed her. Would he fare well through the night? Was he in pain? Why was she still obsessing about him? The monks had the situation under control. Furthermore there was nothing else she could do, and that tore at her heart. A tear fell on her pillow and before long sleep took over.

A loud thump on her door startled Kate and she sat up. How long had she slept?

"Sister Kate, do ye fare well?" a meek voice called out.

Oh thank Heaven it was Sister Mary. Kate sighed in relief. "I be well."

"Abbess Margaret sent me looking for ye. Ye missed the prayer bells again."

Nay, she could not have slept through the prayer bells...could she? "I was a wee bit ill last night but am much better now. I must have needed rest." Kate hated to lie, but no one knew of her little secret and she meant to keep it that way.

"Och, Sister, I'm coming in. Ye need me help."

Kate heard the latch creak and panicked. Mary would never understand the deep cuts on her back, nor the scars of past repentance.

"Nay, Mary, I assure ye I be well. I will be aboot me daily duties in a few minutes." Kate could hear the desperation in Mary's voice. Hopefully she had convinced her enough and Mary would be on her way.

Time stood still as Kate waited for Mary to respond. "Please hurry, I'm quite worried aboot ye."

"Aye, I promise." Kate heard Sister Mary's footsteps move down the corridor and she blew out a deep breath. She winced in pain. Tight skin caked with blood marred her flesh and throbbed down her back. She hadn't intended to lash herself so deeply. Next time she would stay on the path of righteousness.

After Kate gently rinsed the blood off her skin, she applied a salve Abigale had given her. The cream soothed her to the point that she could dress, yet there was still a constant throbbing that reminded her she had not yet been forgiven.

According to what Sister Mary had said, it was time for her to proceed with her daily assessments of the abbey. It was her job to make sure that the abbey was in proper working order, then report back to the abbess, which she wasn't looking forward to doing today.

Kate reviewed her tasks and made a mental note of where she was going to start and where she was going to finish. The kitchen was first on her list: making sure there were enough food supplies and mayhap there would be something left from morning meal to fill her stomach. Then she would make her way to the barn and check on Brother Bim and his goats. Lastly, she needed to check on the progress of the watermill. She would be surprised if any soul was brave enough to take on that daunting task.

But, Kate what about the man in the infirmary. 'Tis yer duty to check on him. Her inner musings were going to drive her daft. Why couldn't she forget about the Highlander? She had brought him to safety, wasn't that enough? It would have to be; she was not going back to the infirmary.

Kate quit her room and plunged into her duties.

6

*T*he kitchen supplies were in order and Kate rewarded her growling belly with a red juicy apple, regardless of the cook's disapproving glare. Her next stop was the goat barn.

Feeling quite accomplished, Kate entered the barn, welcomed by a big gray goat crooning at her. "Brother Bim, are ye here?"

"Och, Sister Kate, it is a pleasure to see ye." The gray-haired monk peered up from a bucket where he was milking a goat.

"Aye, 'tis good to see ye as well. Are there any concerns ye would like me to report back to Abbess Margaret?"

The monk paused. "Nay child, I try to stay far away from that woman. 'Tis best ye do the same." He pointed a crooked index finger at her.

Kate smiled. She knew how to handle the abbess, and apparently she was the only one who could tolerate her.

A soft neigh came from the back of the barn. Unusual, Kate thought. The three horses they had here at the abbey normally stayed in a barn near the watermill, not in the goat pen. Kate walked to the back where a black horse stood tied to a stall wall. As she approached the steed nickered and shook his head up and down as if he recognized her. Kate stuck her hand out and touched his nose. The velvety texture made her smile. She didn't have much experience with horses; in fact she had never ridden one in her six and twenty years of life. Everything she could ever need was right here at Dunfermline Abbey. Why leave?

But there was something about this horse. Indeed there was; it belonged to the injured man. Kate's heart raced at the thought, but as quickly as it began, she doused the fire. *Nay, I won't think of him.*

Although Kate couldn't resist, she still worried about him. Was he still alive? Was he in pain? She shook her head, repulsed at herself. She was weak in allowing her thoughts to drift to temptation and she knew to her core that that man was nothing more than the devil himself luring her in. Yet she had to be strong; she had to fight it.

Back to the task at hand. Kate lifted her chin, turned on her heels, and strode back to the monk milking the goat. "Brother Bim, make sure that horse is penned with the others." She pointed. "Ye know the rules."

Confused at the sudden change in her behavior, Bim continued to tend to his goat. "Aye."

Once outside Kate welcomed the fresh air as she loosened the collar of her dress. What was wrong with her? Mayhap she should go check on the man—clear her conscience. Alas, the prayer bells would be ringing soon and she still needed to make her way to her last task, the watermill. Withal, she was yet under the watchful eye of Abbess Margaret.

Keeping on the covered path, Kate crossed the abbey to the watermill. The sun was out and in the black dress she wore, the rays radiated through the thick wool and became unbearable. Wiping the sweat from her brow, she stopped to observe the mill. The wooden gear's paddles had been destroyed after a storm and since then the watermill had been idle, which meant the production of grinding grain had been halted. Fortunately, the abbey had not suffered much from this inconvenience, but the wheel still needed to be fixed and soon, before the wheat harvest. Because the main wheel was located in the stream, it was a difficult task to fulfill. Kate would be surprised if the watermill ever ran again.

Walking to the water's edge, she bent down and cupped her hands in the stream, then brought them up to her mouth. Her throat stung with thirst and welcomed the coolness of the water. It was hot; indeed summer was on its way. Before Kate could drink her fill, a loud banging brought her attention to the mill. *Is someone here fixing the gear? Odd, the abbess would have mentioned it.*

Drying her hands on her dress, Kate stumbled through the tall grass and up to the mill. The door was cracked open so she peeked in. Stunned at what she saw, she stood breathlessly watching the man from the infirmary vigorously hammering a piece of wood. He took up most of the space inside the mill, and with each smack of the hammer the muscles in his arms twitched with strength. Kate caught herself wondering how those hulking arms would feel wrapped around her. A stream of sweat running down his shirtless chest brought her attention to his wicked physique. With her eyes wide and her heart pounding in her ears, she followed that rippling stream through a red-haired trail below his... *Dear Mother Mary!* His plaid sat low and hugged his hips, fitting him like a second skin.

He was able-bodied and looked as though he had been dropped from the heavens to seduce women from their pure virtue.

Enthralled, Kate completely missed the fact that he had stopped hammering and noticed he had company.

"Och, lass, are ye ill?" He stalked up to her as if she was the prey and he the hunter.

Snapping her eyes to his, she cursed herself for daft. "Aye...nay...I dinnae know." Try as she may she couldn't form a coherent thought with this man so close to her.

The red-headed man bent his head down and gazed into her eyes. "Lass, which is it? Do ye need help or no?"

By the saints, aye she needed help. Temptation was staring her in the face and she had yet to try and fight it. She didn't know what was more shocking, that he was alive, or seeing a man of his stature partly naked.

"Ye...be...alive," Kate stuttered.

"Aye. Ye look as if ye be surprised." The man spun on his heels and strode back to the wood he had been hammering and tugged on his tunic.

Kate could feel her cheeks flush every time he glanced her way. "Please forgive me. I've been terribly rude. I'm Sister Kate." She held out a trembling hand.

The man briefly halted and looked her up and down indifferently as he grabbed another piece of wood. "Hawk."

Retracting her hand, Kate nervously rubbed her palms down her black dress. "'Tis nice to meet ye, Hawk. I assume Abbott Benard knows ye are here and that ye're fixing the watermill?"

"Aye, dinnae fash yerself. I'll be done and headed back home in a few days."

Still shocked, Kate couldn't believe he was alive, and how had he healed so fast? The man had been toying with death two days ago.

"Lass, if ye think I be up to no good, 'tis far from it. I'm a man who repays his debts. The monks in the infirmary saved me life and now I be repaying them by fixing the watermill. Like I said, I will be done in a few days."

A few days? He would be gone? Why did her stomach clench in disappointment? She should be happy that she would be free from his temptation. *Hawk, what a strong name.* She didn't even know this man. *But he's a man of honor, ye do know this much, Kate. He's repaying his debts.* He was a stranger who had appeared out of thin air and caused her safe, guarded world to go spiraling fast out of control. She needed to run as fast and as far away as she could from him.

"Well, then I bid ye a good day. I'm sorry...to have bothered ye." Nervously, Kate quickly turned and opened the door. A blast of fresh air hit her lungs. Ah, fresh air, exactly what she needed. Slamming the door between them, she ran to the path and scurried down the walkway to the dormitory. Prayer bells would be ringing soon and she desperately needed some spiritual intervention before all hope was lost.

∾

*T*he lass had to be daft, Hawk thought as he hammered the two pieces of wood together. Something felt familiar about her, as if he had seen her before. Mayhap it was all in his head. After being at the abbey for two days, he was still trying to see through the fog. Short flashes of recollection came and went, especially at night. A two-headed wyvern with snapping dagger teeth, warning him about an attack, a vision of his sisters running through a throng of chaotic townsfolk, and thick black smoke encircling his body, terrorizing his dragon. Meanwhile his dragon had fallen silent.

Overwhelming emptiness plagued Hawk at the mere thought of forever being without his dragon. He clenched his jaw. What had that damn wyvern done to him? All he knew was that black smoke had damaged him, leaving him powerless, as if he was human. A human? That's exactly how he felt and it made his helpless rage burn. *A weakling.* He spat.

He had been Dragonkine: a mighty immortal dragon with the ability to lay waste to his enemies, to seek and destroy whenever he wanted. Now, instead, he was a mere mortal; his dragon was gone.

Hawk clamped his eyes shut as he dropped his hammer and braced himself for another flood of visions. He was slumped over his horse, pain like never before pounded his body and aching in his bones. And then he was in the infirmary. Rubbing his chest to relieve the throbbing reminded him he wasn't fully healed like he should be. That damn black smoke; what was it and what was it doing to him?

Frustrated, Hawk picked up the wooden paddle he had been hammering and threw it against the wall. Splintered shards of oak burst from the stone wall with a loud crack. Rage filtered throughout and he begged to shift as he paced the floor, thinking about his sisters back at Helmfirth. Had they gotten to the keep in time? Had his men captured the two-headed devil? God's bones, he hoped so. In fact, a vision of the bastard tied to a log, roasting over open flames as his men laughed and drank mead over their victory, brought a brief smirk to his lips.

That triumph was only wishful thinking though. No mortal man could destroy that creature. Hell, even he couldn't kill it. If only he hadn't been caught off guard, he would have shifted and torn both its heads from its foul body.

Feeling out of control for the first time in his life, Hawk broke down. Sorrowfully, he fell to the ground on his knees, balled his fists, and roared his frustration to the sky. He had to get back to Helmfirth; his sisters had to be alive. Running his shaking hands over his hair, he leant back on his heels and slumped his shoulders. Lana and Gwen *had* to be alive.

His breathing slowed as his thoughts faded back to the infirmary. How he got there was a mystery, yet there he'd been, one knock away from death's door. As he lay on a cot, a warm sensation spread across his chest as he felt the tenderness of a soft touch. Restlessly, he had cracked one eye open and saw a women wearing a black veil. A nun? Damn!

As quick as the vision came, it left him. The image was lost, but he could feel the warmth as if he was still being touched. Sweat rolled off his temple as the warmth intensified like the sun shining down on his skin, burning inside him. What in hellfire was happening?

7

"Sister, ye be milking that goat for some time now. I do believe she be empty." Brother Bim studied Kate suspiciously. It wasn't every day that he had help with his goats.

Letting out a deep breath, Kate let go of the goat and wiped her hands. "I'm sorry."

No matter what she did, her mind always wandered to Hawk. Ever since her awkward moment with him, something had changed in her. Her thoughts were always on him. It irritated her no end to not be in control. She was a woman of God and her life was devoted to the abbey, not to lustful musing on a man, a stranger to boot.

Brother Bim, gray and aged, stood and went to Kate, who was still sitting next to the goat. "Child, ye be troubled, aye?"

Kate slouched, defeated. "Ye know me so well, Bim."

There was an uncomfortable silence. Never had she dared to talk about such things before. She had taken a vow, an oath to God. She was in desperate need of guidance before she ran off and did something she would regret. "Have ye ever felt as if ye truly didnae know who ye were? That everything ye stand for no longer defines ye?"

"Och child, are ye telling me ye've come to the fork in the road of life where ye must choose a path?"

Kate nervously wound her hands together, never meeting meeting his gaze. She wouldn't be able to take the disappointment in Bim's eyes after she told him the truth. "I feel as though I be lost, Bim. My soul feels restless." Purposely she left out one small detail; she wanted to leave the abbey. But knowing Bim, he already knew.

Brother Bim took Kate's hands in his. She looked up at him and prayed that the wise man could lead her back to the path of right-eousness she'd tread before Hawk had entered her world. "Ye see, Kate, there comes a time in yer life when ye must find yer true call-ing. Sometimes it be right in front of ye, and other times ye must seek it out on yer own. A spiritual pilgrimage some would say. I say 'tis the next chapter in yer life."

She sat searching his eyes as if everything he was saying made perfectly good sense. "But how, Bim, how do I know where to go or what to do when I dinnae know meself? It feels wrong of me to think of a life outside these abbey walls." And there, she had said it. Didn't sound as daft as she thought it would.

It seemed like forever, waiting for Brother Bim's reaction. He was the only monk at the abbey who loved her as though she was his own daughter. He was the one who brought her inside the abbey from the gatehouse the day her mother had abandoned her. It was Bim who took care of her, fed her, scolded her, and kept the monsters at bay at night. It was Bim who had taken on the role of father and she loved him dearly. Being a disappointment in his eyes would ruin her.

Bim pressed his lips together and sternly gazed at Kate. "I can 'no give ye the answers ye seek. 'Tis only ye who can find yer own happi-ness in life, yer calling. But have no doubt; ye've served God and this abbey well. I believe ye already know the answer."

What? This was daft. How could it be? If she knew what to do she wouldn't be here seeking his words of wisdom. If she knew what to do, she wouldn't be here brooding in her indecisiveness. Frustrated, she exhaled.

Out of breath, Sister Mary came running into the barn with two baskets of food. "I be terrible sorry I'm late. We are shorthanded in the kitchen this eve." Winded, she pressed on. "Sister Ann's stomach ails her and Brother Tom is making a mess oot of me kitchen." She placed one of the baskets down on a stool for Bim. He never ate with the rest of the monks in the dining hall; he preferred his goats' company.

Sister Kate stood. "Och Mary, I'm done here. What can I help ye with?"

"I have to deliver this basket to the man at the mill. Would ye be so kind and take it to him?"

"Well, I—I—"

"Oh thank ye, Sister." She shoved the basket into Kate's hands and quit the barn.

Kate looked at Bim and they shared a smile. Perhaps he was right. If she searched deep enough she would know what to do. Yet did she have the courage to go forward? Could she trust herself to make the right decision or, by the same token, could she trust a stranger?

Grabbing the basket, she started for the watermill. Along the way she made up her mind; she was going to leave the abbey. All of her life she had felt as though she did not truly belong here. Her soul indeed was restless and it was time for her to find her own place in the world instead of following righteous rule. But leaving the safety of the abbey wasn't a decision to take lightly. Everything she had ever known was within these walls. Security and her vow to God kept her here, but curiosity and the desire to seek her own way in life drove her further beyond the comforts she had as a nun.

But with no coin, no horse, nor tradable goods, it was going to be a difficult task. If only she had one piece of fine jewelry. Wrapping her fingers around her locket a thought passed through her mind. Perhaps she could trade her mother's necklace. Nay, it was the only thing she had of hers. There was no way she could part with it.

Then she remembered; Hawk was going to leave here...soon. Why not ask him to escort her to the nearest village, or mayhap his? Yet she knew no one and it was unsafe to be a woman alone in an unfamiliar village. Add to that the fact that it was inappropriate for her to escape into the Highlands with a man. But how else was she going to leave? If only Abigale had been here, she would know what to do.

Kate paused in mid stride. "That's it. Abigale." She would ask Hawk to escort her to Black Stone on the Hill. She would be safe there and knew she would be welcomed with open arms.

Kate smiled. For the first time she had taken control and reined in her indecision. It empowered her and gave her hope. Now she had to persuade Hawk.

A wee bit eager, she rapped on the door of the mill. The door cracked open and she peeked inside. "Hawk!" she called out. There was no answer. Opening the door wider, she stepped inside. Candles were burning, filling the room with a yellow glow. Searching the room, Kate noticed all of the wood was gone, and the area was clean and tidy. Where was he? Was she too late and he was gone? Her heart plummeted into her stomach. "Hawk!"

The air in the room thickened and turned hot as she heard footsteps behind her. Her body stiffened and the hairs on the back of her neck bristled. He was behind her; she knew it, could feel it, yet she couldn't will her body to turn around.

"What are ye doing here, Sister Kate?"

His deep voice hummed through her body like a soothing lullaby that made her shiver. She tried to answer him, but her throat went dry.

Hawk bent down and pressed his lips into her black veil just below her ear. "Sister, are ye going to answer me?"

She closed her eyes. This man knew exactly what he was doing to her, making her squirm under his fiery gaze. His warm breath set her skin ablaze. Even through the woolen veil she could feel him. *Kate, if ye want to leave the abbey, concentrate.* When Kate opened her eyes and turned to face Hawk, she found herself pressed against his massive chest. Slowly her eyes met his intense stare and she bit her bottom lip nervously.

Breaking the spellbound trance she was under, Kate looked away from those smoldering depths and walked over to the wooden table. "I...I brought food." She unpacked the basket.

Kate placed a plate down with bread and cheese when she realized that Hawk hadn't followed her to the table. "Are ye hungry? Sister Mary makes the finest bread." She smiled.

Silent, Hawk walked over and sat down at the table.

"Do ye mind if I join ye?"

Hawk motioned for her to sit. As she did, she poured him a tankard of mead, for she was going to need all the help she could get to convince Hawk to take her with him when he left. "Ye've done a fine job on the watermill. Brother Bim said it be the best work he has seen in ages."

Ripping off a hunk of bread, he popped it in his mouth. "I kept me word," he said indifferently.

Kate sat and studied him for a while, watching his strong jaws chew through the bread. She watched him lick the mead from his lips when he drank. Everything about him intrigued her, she could watch him forever. Mayhap her whole plan was a mistake. Trusting herself around this man was going to be her downfall; she knew it.

Though if she was going to jaunt off into the Highlands with this stranger, she needed to know him better. Unfortunately, Hawk was a man of few words, which meant she had to get him to talk.

~

Time passed and not a word was spoken by either of them. Uncomfortable silence filled the room. Hawk studied the lass across from him with a watchful eye.

"Can I ask ye a question?" Kate asked.

Absolutely not. Questions only lead to trouble and Hawk wanted nothing to do with trouble. Helmfirth was in enough turmoil; he sure as hell didn't need a lass's troubles on top of it. Withal, he had questions of his own.

"Why?" He answered with a mouth full of food.

"I'm curious." She shrugged her shoulders. "'Tis all."

"Ye might no' like what ye hear, Sister.'Tis best ye keep yer questions to yerself."

"Where are ye from?"

Finishing his mead, he placed the tankard on the table and glared at her. The lass needed to learn when to keep her mouth closed. This was the problem with lasses, they always questioned everything. "Lass, ye no listen verra well. I told ye, no questions."

"Well, if I recall correctly, ye mentioned I would no' like what I hear. Ye said nothin' aboot me no' asking a question."

Hawk wiped his mouth with the back of his hand and pinned her harshly with his green eyes. He leaned back into his chair and crossed his arms over his chest. She wasn't going to take no for an answer, was she? "Go on then, ask yer question."

Kate leaned forward. "Where are ye from?"

"I'm the Laird of Helmfirth."

"When I found ye outside of the abbey walls ye were badly injured. What happened?"

Taken aback, he sat up. "Ye...ye're the one who took me to the infirmary, are ye not?" Indeed it had to be her. From the moment he had walked into the mill he had felt her warmth. The same warmth that throbbed in his chest now.

"Aye, me and Brother Tom." Kate shyly tucked a piece of unbound hair behind her veil.

He wished he had all the pieces to the puzzle, but he was still struggling through the fog. "I was attacked back home, and the next thing I knew, I was waking up here in the infirmary surrounded by monks telling me I was lucky to be alive."

"What about yer family? Did they survive?"

Hawk tore his gaze from hers before she drew him in further. He leaned back. "Eat. Ye ask too many questions."

"I'm sorry, Hawk, I—"

"How aboot ye? What aboot yer family?" Quickly he changed the topic.

Kate fidgeted with a piece of bread in her hands. "The abbey has been me family since I was a wee babe. My mother left me here."

Hawk clenched his jaw tight, knowing exactly how it felt to be abandoned. A mother was supposed to love her children forever.

Before he could say a word, Kate continued, "The abbey has been good to me." She smiled.

And there it was, a lass's smile, the one thing that could draw a man in and bring him to his knees. When a lass flashed a smile she was always up to no good. His sisters had taught him that trick. Sister Kate was up to something. Why else would she have stayed? Surely it wasn't because she was hungry or fancied his company. "Why do I feel ye have something other than me well being on yer mind, Sister?"

"I did no'—I"

"Dinnae be shy, tell me."

Kate looked down into her lap. "I want to leave the abbey."

Confused by her confession, Hawk didn't see that it had anything to do with him. "And why do ye want to leave?"

"Hawk." She spoke his name so softly. *Aye, this lass wants something.* "I want ye to take me to Black Stone on the Hill."

He flew out of his seat. "What! Nay!"

"Please listen before ye say no. Ye know what 'tis like to have yer freedom. To make yer own decisions. I do no'. I've had no choice but to stay here obeying every rule, having all my decisions made for me, and staying on a path that I dinnae wish to take anymore. I need me freedom. I want to pursue my life without judgment."

Hawk paused. He could see tears filling her eyes and her cheeks were flushed. A lass's desperate plea, tears. Nay, there was no way he was going to take her away from the abbey.

"Kate, ye took a vow, an oath to God. I can no' do it. I won't."

There was silence between them except for his heavy footsteps heading over to the small window overlooking the stream. Hawk took in the view. Dark blue water glistened under the moonlight and he wished he had left the abbey sooner like he had planned to do. Who the hell was he fooling? His soul had been damned years ago. He hadn't a righteous bone in his body. But that didn't mean he would be the one to help Sister Kate break her vows. Even if he were to look past them, he could not risk her life and take her through the Highlands. With no weapons and no dragon, how was he supposed to defend himself, let alone Kate?

A soft touch on his shoulder startled him and he closed his eyes. Aye, she was persistent.

"I'm sorry to have upset ye. Please understand I just want a chance to be happy wherever that may be. My soul is restless here."

Hawk turned around and met deep hazel eyes gazing up at him. He could see the yearning in them and, in fact, he did understand her desire for freedom. God's bones, what was he going to do with the lass?

A reaction he had no control over took him by surprise. He cupped her face and held her stare. "Ye took an oath, Kate. Do ye understand what ye be asking of me?"

"Aye, I do, and this is my decision."

He held firm, glaring into the softness of her eyes. Reason after reason told him to walk away, that this lass was not his problem. But that nagging pull as if she had reached out and drawn him inside her, wouldn't let him be. If he didn't accept her proposal, she would place her trust with the wrong person, a man with ill intentions perhaps. He could not very well live with that on his conscience.

Quickly he let her go, walked back to the table and began to eat, dismissing her as if their moment had never happened. "Ye'll need yer own horse."

"Aye." Kate joined him at the table.

"We leave tomorrow night. When the moon is fullest."

"Aye."

He peered at her once more with a stern gaze. "And dinnae be late. I won't wait for ye. Understand?"

"Aye."

They sat in silence. Hawk didn't dare another glance at Kate, but he could feel her eyes on him, smiling. *Fool!* What had he just done?

8

*H*awk tightened his saddle for the fifth time as he anxiously waited for Kate's arrival. His horse gave an irritated huff. Patting his stallion on its hindquarters, apologizing to the fine steed, Hawk kept a lookout for Kate outside the gatehouse. Apprehensive about the whole situation, he wouldn't be surprised if she didn't come. He hoped he'd called her bluff, that she had changed her mind and decided to stay at the abbey. But there was too much desperation in her eyes; she wanted her independence and was willing to do anything for it. Thank Christ, she had asked him and not some wandering traveler willing to take advantage of an innocent. Even though he didn't want to be responsible for the lass leaving the nunnery, he understood her desperate plea. Besides, it was her choice.

Looking up at the clouds passing by a bright moon, Hawk thought her chance was passing by. He was serious; he would leave here without her. He had warned her not to be late. The longer he stayed out here in the open, the quicker he would be caught and questioned about his motives.

Horse hooves clopped down the cloister, bringing his attention to the gatehouse. Hawk strode there and abruptly stopped. It was Kate.

Her black veil was gone. Hawk's heart paused; with the veil gone, he could see she had beautiful short brown hair that framed her petite round face. Lovely, elegant, and innocent. He was in trouble.

Holding back the urge to go to her, he saw her stop right before the threshold. Why wasn't she moving? She stood staring at the ground as if she might be having second thoughts. Indeed this wasn't an easy task for her, leaving the safety of the abbey and everything she had ever known, to enter into a new world that was unlike anything she had ever seen or experienced, so he allowed her a moment to collect her thoughts. He couldn't blame her; this first step past the abbey walls was one she would never forget. Hawk stood, watching, waiting for Kate to say she was ready to leave. He hoped it would be soon; getting caught was something he didn't want to chance.

Hawk held Kate's stare as she looked at him from across the threshold, as if she sought his approval, his encouragement. He watched her take a deep breath then cross the barrier into wickedness. His heart ached for her, for he knew how cruel the world could be, and for some unknown reason, a sickening feeling hit him like a blade to the gut; he would be her downfall. If he wasn't careful he would ruin her. Looking at her he could see that she held him to a higher standard, like a hero. And Hawk was no hero.

Kate approached and he took the reins from her. "'Tis aboot time," he chided.

"Ye said when the moon was the brightest. "'Tis bright, no?" Kate brushed her hair back behind her ears nervously.

"Never mind." Hawk checked her saddle for tightness and was alarmed at how loose the thing was. Did she not have any experience with horses? "Kate, do ye go around riding yer horse like this?"

"What do ye mean? I put a saddle on her the best I know how." She shrugged her shoulders indifferently.

He grunted. "If ye go ridin' a horse like this, ye're bound to fall off. Yer saddle is too loose."

Kate stood quietly as she looked beyond him into the forest they were about to journey through.

Hawk tightened the saddle and gave it a good shove, reassuring himself that the damn thing was secure. "Ye never know who or what ye're going to run into in the Highlands. Surely you don't want to slide off your horse when something is chasing you."

"What do ye mean by 'something'?"

"I told ye the Highlands are no' safe. Ye have to be on alert at all times and ready to run when need be."

Kate shrugged him off again. "I'll be fine."

That he wasn't too sure of, because he could see straight through her false façade.

A black strap hung freely from inside her satchel, which piqued Hawk's interest. He opened the leather sack and pulled out a whip. His brows furrowed. Confused, he looked at the leather straps dangling at the end of a rounded handle. "And what might this be?" He held up the whip.

Kate gasped. "This is no business of yers. Ye have no right rummaging through me belongings." She stormed over to him and snatched the leather straps from him.

Hawk grabbed her wrist and pulled her against his chest. He pinned her sternly with his green eyes. "Aye, I do. I need to know if ye are of sound mind. I will no' jaunt through the Highlands with a daft woman. I won't be held responsible."

She lifted her chin and squared her shoulders. "I assure ye, my laird, I am of sound mind and that's all ye need to know." Ripping her wrist from his grasp, she took the flogger and slipped it back into her satchel.

Hawk stood dumfounded. *Bloody Hell! What is she doing with such an object as that?* He was going to have to keep a close eye on her. By her reaction, she had some demons of her own.

~

*K*ate fidgeted with her satchel, not because it was misplaced, but because she couldn't stand to look at Hawk right now. He'd crossed the line. How dare he go through her things? Kate had never felt so violated in her life. They were called personal items for a reason.

As she stewed, two large hands wrapped around her waist and he hoisted her up on top of her horse. She looked down at Hawk, who paid her no mind. She huffed and looked ahead waiting for him to mount and lead the way. She prayed he wouldn't't notice that she had never ridden a horse before. Telling him that wee bit of information was irrelevant after what he'd done.

They rode in silence. Hawk led the way over the thick grassy forest floor while Kate followed closely, taking in the scenery. The moon lit up the sky, cascading rays down through the tall treetops as their branches danced to the sway of the wind. Kate shivered and pulled her cloak tighter around her shoulders. The horses felt the briskness of the wind, as their tails swished back and forth.

Being unfamiliar with the Highlands, Kate didn't know what to expect. The terrain, which had started out smooth, quickly turned rough. The trail was narrow and muddy from what she could tell in the moonlight. She kept her eyes in front of her, closely watching Hawk. He rode his horse down the dirt path as if he knew the Highlands like the back of his hand. Kate noticed a difference in him, the deeper they rode into the glen. His broad shoulders relaxed a bit, yet his eyes were on alert, scanning the trees and thickets of bushes.

It was well into the early morn when the mist covered the low-lying valley as the sun roused the sky in light orange hues over the mountaintops. Kate had never seen the sky look so beautiful; it took her breath away. The striking view engulfed her, for she didn't realize that her horse had stopped and was chewing on a blade of grass.

"'Tis a bonny morn, aye?" Hawk rode up and stopped next to her, taking in the dawn.

Surprised to hear his voice so close, Kate swiftly looked over her shoulder at him. In this view, in the Highlands, and right at this moment, Hawk looked to be at peace. He was purely in his environment. "Aye, I've no' seen a more beautiful dawn." Kate smiled and continued taking in the magic of the Highlands.

Was it the splendor of the glen that made the morn feel so perfect in every way? Mayhap it was that, for the first time in her life, she was on her own, making her own decisions? Or was it the man next to her making her dreams come true? Even though she had been madder than a wet cat at him, at this moment she couldn't help but think that life as simple as it stood right now, was perfect.

"Kate, we need to keep moving." Hawk motioned for her to follow as he started back down the trail they were on. She tugged on the reins, trying to get her horse's mouth away from the grass. The horse pulled back and resisted. "Let's go, girl. 'Tis time to go," Kate commanded softly. Apparently the mare's stomach outweighed Kate's orders, for the gray, dappled beast kept eating away. Annoyed at the game her horse was playing, Kate exhaled, then looked to see if Hawk saw what was happening. She didn't want him to know how inexperienced she was. It would only make things worse. He was already suspicious of her. *Why won't this horse move?*

Kate leaned forward and whispered. "Please, Ninny, move," she begged.

A loud boisterous laugh bellowed in front of her as she peered up and saw Hawk laughing at her. With haste, Kate straightened herself in the saddle and tipped her chin up. "She's hungry."

All laughing aside, Hawk nonchalantly halted his black mare beside Ninny. He leaned over to her and Kate could feel her pulse quicken. "Ye have to be firm and tell her what ye want, Kate." A shiver ran down her spine as she felt his warm breath glide across her skin below her ear. She turned her head towards him and her gaze fell upon his thick neck. She watched a vein pump rhythmically in tune with her own heart. She could feel the intensity of his stare warming her body. Her eyes dared to go farther and took in his masculine jawline brushed with red hairs. His jaw clenched as she met his green eyes. He licked his lips and her whole body went numb. If she was any hotter she would melt right here in the saddle.

Forget about the horse. Kate wanted to tell him what she was thinking. She wanted her first kiss to be from him. She wanted to feel the smoothness of his lips on hers. She wanted him to teach her how to be thoroughly kissed. Before she knew what her body was doing, she closed her eyes, waiting for his mouth to touch hers.

Without as much as a warning, Hawk slapped the mare on the hind end and got her attention. She flung her head up and pranced as if the slap had stung.

In disbelief Kate's eyes shot open and she quickly regained control of the horse. Mother Mary, she needed to control her lustful thoughts. Hawk smirked and shook his head as he rode past her and picked the trail back up. Clearly she had misread him, and now she felt like a fool, a wanton fool. A man of his stature could have any woman he wanted. For all she knew he could have a wife back home, and here she was acting as if she knew what he desired. Surely it wasn't a kiss from her. If she was going to survive she was going to have to resist temptation and focus on her life.

Passing the long hours into the evening with a rest here and there, Kate refused to let her thoughts rest on the man in front of her. Focusing on her future, she couldn't wait to arrive at Black Stone on the Hill. Never having been in a castle before, she thought how different it would be compared to abbey life. No prayer bells constantly ringing throughout all the hours of the night. She could make her own paths instead of the ones she was told to take, but most of all she would be able to come and go as she pleased.

Also she wondered how Abigale would react to her leaving Dunfermline and the nunnery after twenty-and-six years. Hopefully she wouldn't think her daft. Then there was sweet Jamie; she couldn't wait to squeeze her. But the image that made her happy, yet scared all at the same time, was knowing a new beginning awaited her. Whatever it might be, she was in control of her own destiny.

She didn't dare ask any questions when Hawk stopped in front of her without telling her what he was doing. Normally if they were stopping for rest, he would say so. Hawk dismounted and walked off the beaten path. She followed him with her eyes as far as she could before he disappeared. What was he up to? She tried not to panic, but she couldn't help but worry. "Hawk!" she called out.

Shortly he returned. "We'll camp here tonight." Taking her reins, he led the horse deep into the forest to a clearing. Kate looked around. There was no shelter, just a wide-open space with a few trees. "We camp, here? Oot in the open?"

Hawk began removing his rolled up blanket from his horse. "Aye."

At first, Kate was reluctant to dismount but she finally did and was relieved to be off her horse and to stretch her legs. With her hands on her back she stretched her neck from side to side. "Hawk, are ye sure this is a safe place to make camp?"

"Lass, ye be in the Highlands. Do ye have a better suggestion?" He shoved his rolled up blanket into her chest. "Ye make camp. I'll find us something to start a fire with."

After Kate had laid down their blankets and Hawk had started a flaming fire, they ate bread and drank mead in an uncomfortable silence. Kate looked across the red and orange flames at Hawk as he bit off a hunk of bread, wishing that he would say something to keep her mind from wandering about. She was going to go daft if he didn't say something soon. With the night approaching fast, animal sounds echoed through the forest, sending her imagination wild. She needed him to talk to her to get her mind off the lurking beasties waiting to pounce. "How long until we reach Black Stone?"

Sitting with his arms resting on his knees, Hawk looked as if he was far away in thought. "Kate, there's been a change in plans."

"What do ye mean?"

"We'll be in Helmfirth by tomorrow eve."

"But ye said—"

"Lass, I know what I said, and I'll take ye to Black Stone, but first I must go home."

She couldn't believe what she was hearing. Had this been trickery all along? Her heart raced alongside her mind. Had she made her first mistake in trusting him? Then again, there was nothing in this deal for him. She had no coin to give, nothing to barter with. Calming her nerves, Kate pressed on. "Well, I'm sure ye want to be home. Surely yer wife and family have missed ye."

Choking on a piece of bread, he shot her a stern glare. "I have no wife nor children."

Taken aback and feeling the slightest bit of relief, Kate smiled. "Are ye alright?"

"I'm well." Hawk cleared his throat. "I have two sisters back home and I need to make sure they fare well."

"Are they in some kind of trouble?"

"Kate, ye ask too many questions. Get some sleep." Hawk stretched out on his blanket and closed his eyes, indicating the conversation was over.

She watched him for a while. She wanted to inquire deeper into his world, but she knew better than to pry. A rustle disturbed a nearby bush, causing her to jump. "Did ye hear that noise?"

"Haud yer wheesht. Go. To. Sleep," Hawk gritted through his teeth and rolled over onto his side. "Whatever it is won't hurt ye."

Kate huffed and lay down, pulling the blanket up to her chin. Her eyes were wide open, surveying the tree line, searching for any signs of beasties. Every sound she heard startled her and her imagination took flight. There was no hope for sleep tonight. Because she was out in the Highlands with a man and forest creatures, sleep would pass her by. If only she could quiet her mind, mayhap she would make it through the night.

9

*I*t was a beautiful day at Black Stone on the Hill. Outside the sun shined down on Clan Douglas as they danced in joy, celebrating two lives becoming one. As soon as Conall and Effie said 'I do', the music hummed and the feast began. When a Dragonkine found his mate, it was always a grand occasion.

Magnus, the elder of the Dragonkine, sat down at one of the tables covered in heather and watched the festivities. Conall picked up his lovely wife and spun her around as if he was showing her off to the world. Abigale, the laird's wife and princess of Scotland, danced with her adoptive daughters, Flora and Annis, with her wee babe Jamie in her arms. Alice, who was much more than a kitchen maid and more of a mother to the laird, hummed to the music as she made sure that all the provisions were displayed on the tables properly. She nodded at Magnus and he gave her a wink in satisfaction. Magnus smiled; indeed it was a glorious day.

Yet there was always a lingering feeling of dread in his gut. Since returning from the dragon elders' realm, he knew that the Dragonkine warriors were living targets waiting for attack. The earth shook, a constant reminder that King Drest had been awakened.

Magnus experienced every quake pulse through his veins, feeling the king's ferocity as he clawed the earth's wall with unwavering determination to seek out his revenge on the humans. Magnus had hoped the king would never become unearthed.

"Magnus, auld man," James Douglas said as he took the seat next to the Dragonkine elder, "What be on yer mind?"

Magnus exhaled. "Time is getting close, I can feel it."

Looking at his beautiful wife, James watched her dance with his children, with the same terrible awareness as his elder. "I feel it too. I've sent Rory to Helmfirth to warn their people. Caden leaves in the morn to Ravenloch to do the same. I pray that we aren't too late."

"Aye, we must protect Govan from Marcus. He can no' succeed."

The plan that Laird Douglas was executing was to protect the borderlands and clans surrounding Govan. It was the holy land where Drest and his seven royals had been tricked by MacAlpin and now lay underground until pure dragon blood was spilled. With Marcus alive it was only a matter of time before the king rose and brought with him hell on earth.

Now that Marcus had chosen his side, it left six remaining Dragonkine warriors. That was if the Laird of Helmfirth was still alive. No one knew where his loyalties lay since he stayed isolated from his dragon brethren. Adding to the danger, James and Conall had more to lose; they had human wives and children. King Robert had been kind to them. Rory, on the other hand, had voiced his opinion on more than one occasion that Dragonkine should have their own king and follow the alpha as they were destined to do.

Aye, with the awakening of King Drest, loyalties would be tested and the Kine could be destroyed. Scotland was in grave danger and Magnus could do nothing about it but sit and wait for the enemy to make a move.

James scratched his jaw, irritated at feeling so hopeless. "I wish I knew where the bastards were. I wish there was more I could do."

"Och, lad, ye're protecting the surrounding areas the best ye can. When the Devil wants something, he takes. There's no stopping that kind of evil. Drest will come. We must fight back and protect the ones we love with our lives."

They sat in silence and watched the clan members dance and celebrate the day. James stood and clasped a hand on Magnus's shoulder. "Today we be merry, for tomorrow is unknown." He smiled and joined Abigale and the girls.

Magnus smiled and agreed; today life was good. Drinking the last of his mead, he left the table and was in search of more drink, when he spotted something moving behind a thicket of blackthorn on the forest's edge. His body hummed and sweat beaded on his forehead. His dragon growled from deep inside his core, not because he wanted to shift; he wanted to claim.

Notably inquisitive, Magnus strode to the thicket with his hand on the hilt of his broadsword. Whoever or whatever it was must have seen him coming and fled. Picking up his pace, he reached the forest and turned around, searching for any kind of movement. Out of the corner of his eye he saw the hem of a white dress whip in the wind behind a tree. It was her.

Crouching down with his sword drawn, he attentively approached the tree. The crunching of dead leaves alerted her and she fled from her hiding place, running deeper into the forest. Magnus sheathed his sword and charged after the lass.

Long, chestnut hair trailed behind her as she raced with all her might; however, in one long stride, Magnus captured his quarry. Reaching out, he grabbed the woman by her slender waist and brought her to the ground on top of him, breaking her fall. They rolled until she lay on her back and the Highlander pinned her arms above her head, surprised that she didn't fight him.

Straddling the woman, Magnus brushed her hair away from her face. "Bloody Hell! 'Tis ye?" His brows furrowed as he glowered at her. A familiar thought flashed as he remembered the lass. Then again, how could he forget? She'd saved his life.

Her hair was covered in brown leaves and her once-white dress was now dirt-stained. Her chest rapidly rose up and down as she tried to catch her breath. "'Tis me. We need to talk, Magnus."

Magnus stood, helping the lass up. "It was ye who halted the Creepers when I left the elders' lair, wasn't it?"

"Aye, I did."

"Why would ye have risked yer life?"

"'Tis much more, I'm afraid. I've been running from those bastards for years. But now something more precious to me could be in danger and I need yer help."

"Why me?"

"Do ye remember that night at the tavern twenty-and-six summers ago?" The woman brushed her hands down her hair and it turned into a fair blonde, then she covered her eyes and when she revealed them, the once brown eyes were now midnight blue.

Stunned, Magnus took a step back and shook his head in disbelief. "Ye told me ye were a bar maid, not a—"

"Dargonkine female." She took a step closer. "I be terribly sorry for misleading ye. I truly am. But I had me reasons, please believe me."

"I dinnae know what to believe." Magnus took a step back and stroked his long, red beard. The woman he'd met years ago in the tavern had never left his thoughts. One night with this woman had been the best damn night he had ever experienced in his long immortal life. But when he awoke in the morn, she had left. Not only had she stung his pride, she'd left a hole in his heart.

"Och, I see I have come to ye for naught." The lass shook her head and her chestnut hair and brown eyes returned to normal. Turning on her heels, she walked away, but stilled when a strong hand on her arm pulled her back.

"Lass, ye went to great measures to seek oot me help. What aren't ye telling me?"

She glanced down at her muddy shoes. "We have a daughter, Magnus." She looked up him. "She's in danger. We must find her."

The urgency in her voice pulled at his heart, or was it the realization that he had a daughter? Whatever it was, curiosity had the best of him. Having King Drest to deal with was enough to endure, but with this newfound information, Magnus didn't know what to think.

"What kind of danger is she in?"

"The Creepers, death, will be after her if they're no' already." Desperate tears rolled down her cheeks and she fought back heavy sobs. "Magnus, we must find her."

Magnus pulled the lass into a loving embrace. At one time he had searched for her. He had dared to want more, but fate turned out differently. She'd escaped him and now he wanted to know why. *Why does she hide her identity? Why didn't she tell me about the babe?* There were too many unanswered questions; he couldn't turn the lass down.

Anger prevailed at the thought that this woman had lied to him, keeping their daughter a secret. Even though she said she had her reasons, no excuse was good enough for keeping his own blood from him. He cared naught about the lass; he cared more about his daughter, and if in fact she was in danger, it would take a dragon to get her out of it. In time he'd get the woman to tell him everything about their night together and where she had been all these years; however his daughter was his first priority.

He swept away her tears and held her stare. "I'll help ye find our daughter, but ye will answer me questions along the way. Understand?"

"Aye, I will tell ye everything. I promise," she sniffled.

"Good, because I'm too angry with ye to argue." Magnus broke their embrace. "Stay here. I will be back with horses and food."

"Aye."

After he informed James that he had personal business to attend to, without describing every detail, for he still had pieces of the puzzle missing himself, he fled to the kitchen, staying clear of Alice. She always had a way of getting the truth out of you and, frankly, he was in no mood to be truthful. He had no idea how long they would be gone as he packed a burlap bag full of loaves of bread, cheese, and a skin of mead.

Flinging the bag onto his saddle and securing it with a tight pull, he mounted his steed and quit the stables. He purposely left with only one horse. It turned out after all that he trusted her as much as she trusted himself around a fine lass—not one bit. Mayhap he did have other intentions after all. A beautiful Dragonkine female pressed up against his cock as they rode through the Highlands would be a fine torture to endure. He smiled wickedly and pushed his steed with haste to the forest, hoping she would still be waiting for him.

10

"What do ye mean, a dragon chased ye away from Helmfirth?" Marcus towered over Tavish, the wyvern, now in human form and still winded from the chase. He stood with his head down in shame for failing to burn down Helm-firth. "A green dragon swept by me from oot of nowhere and took me by surprise, my laird."

Marcus irately paced the ice cave, scratching his jaw.

"My laird, if I may continue, I did kill the Red Hawk before the dragon appeared."

Marcus paused.

"Aye, I killed him with me black magic. He be a threat no longer."

A smile slowly crept across Marcus's face. The Red Hawk was dead. He wasn't a fool after all for saving Tavish's life, now was he? Indeed the bastard's black magic came in handy when dealing with these Dragonkine fools. Though he must tread softly, for he wanted no part of that black smoke, with his dragon growing stronger every day. "Ye did well, Tavish. Do ye have his blood?"

"Och. My laird, I...I" As Tavish scrambled for an excuse, he gave Marcus the good news first. "I was able to gather a few Helmfirth filth who were hiding in the woods for slaves. Yer Creepers are holding them captive in tents at the bottom of the mountain."

Marcus squeezed Tavish's shoulder. "How are we supposed to waken our Lord without dragon blood?" he seethed in his ear.

Tavish stood on shaking knees. "Hawk vanished, but...I...I know he's dead."

At that moment Marcus shushed the blubbering idiot and called himself a fool for trusting this incapable wyvern.

The slightest sweet fragrance swept across the cave. Marcus turned his head to the opening of the cavern and breathed in deeply the cold mountain air. A hum vibrated about his body and raced through his veins as he stepped closer to the mouth of the ice cave, astonished. That scent rang out loud and clear, a Dragonkine female.

When one door closes opportunity knocks on another. He smirked. Taking in another fulfilling lungful of sweetness, he forged his plan, but in a new direction. On the morrow he would find that female. Not only could he smell her, but he could feel the power she possessed. King Drest would need a female to return him to his full strength.

"That will be all." Marcus excused Tavish with a wave of his hand and returned to the back of the cave.

A beautiful Dragonkine female wrapped in furs and hidden behind strands of honey-colored hair sat in the corner. Her right ankle was cuffed to a metal chain that was attached to the ice wall, but was long enough so she could stand. Marcus bent down in front of her and brushed her hair from her face. The female drew her legs up tighter to her body and slapped his hands away.

Her actions didn't anger him. He always got what he wanted, whether she approved of it or not. The Creepers knew he needed strength, and to regain his dragon, so bringing this beauty to him had been wise; it was exactly what he needed. Even though he had fought the gift at first, he now craved her power.

"Ye know I won't hurt ye unless ye misbehave." Marcus ran the back of his icy hand down her cheek and felt her quiver.

"Please, let me go." The female's voice shook.

Marcus removed his hand, stunned that she had spoken. His body tensed as her soothing voice rippled through him. She hadn't muttered one word to him since the creeper brought her to the cave, nor did he know her name. "Och lass, ye speak. Tell me yer name."

The female held his stare as if she could see straight into his soul. "If ye do no' let me go, then there is no need for ye to know me name."

"Ye know I can no' let ye go. Ye're mine. 'Tis rude to return a gift." Marcus smirked.

"Then I am dead. Call me what ye wish, for I'm no longer the woman I used to be." The female turned her head and looked to the back of the cave.

There was a small, minuscule part of him that felt for the lass. She was being held here against her will and forced to heal him. Healing a monster alone had to be devastating, but she had to know that once he awakened their true king, their world would be whole again. Even though all Dragonkine believed their females had been slaughtered or enslaved to the point of extinction, she was important in the rebuilding of her kind.

Marcus roughly grabbed the female by the chin and forcefully pulled her head forward so she had to look at him. "Understand one thing, female. The king is coming and ye'll want to be on me side when he returns to Earth to reclaim what is rightfully his. Ye'll bear me children and ye'll tell me what happened to the rest of the females."

She snapped her head from his grip. "I'll die first. Ye're a fool to think the king will —"

Rage took over Marcus and he slapped the female to shut her up. No one ever again would call him a fool. "Be careful what ye wish for, lass." Marcus stood and walked away. In no time at all she could bring out the wickedness in him. In a way he liked it; it made him feel alive. He hadn't meant to hit her, but calling him a fool was a huge mistake, a mistake that she would never make again.

11

*E*arly morn broke through the graying clouds, yet the sun still slept. In a slumber-filled daze, Hawk rolled over to find he wasn't alone. A soft, warm body stirred as it snuggled next to him, finding warmth. Without knowing what he was doing, he pulled the figure closer and was flooded with the sweet smell of heather. The scent engulfed him and hummed through his body, reminding him of when he was a child. At night when the wind blew across the moor, the smell of heather would fill his childhood bedchamber.

Breathing in deeper, Hawk felt soft breasts press against his chest. Aye, female. He brought up his hand and caressed her cheek, marveling at its smoothness. She was divine. Craving more of this enchantment, he traced his finger across her jawline and down her neck. The woman stretched her head back, giving him full access to her slender neck as if she begged for more of his touch. A faint pleasurable moan sent a jolt of awareness straight to his cock. This had to be a dream.

"Hawk," she whispered.

Dreams never felt this real. His eyes flew open, whilst the sleep fog rolled off. The forest trees came into view and the songbirds chirped their morn tunes. He realized where he was and whose neck he was nuzzling—Kate's. Wrapped in a blanket, she nestled next to him.

Bloody Hell! Had they…Nay, he would never have taken her to bed, and furthermore, he would have remembered it. Hawk peeked under the blanket and was pleasantly pleased to see them both fully clothed. She must have come to him sometime during the night. He looked over to the smoldering fire. Aye, she must have been cold.

Trying not to wake her, he slowly removed his arms from around her. He didn't want her to wake and find them in this awkward position. It would frighten her and he didn't need any more awkwardness between them. A long journey still lay ahead.

Slowly he slid away from their embrace as Kate stretched. She yawned and fussed with her hair while waking up. Hawk stood and paced back and forth. What was wrong with him? He reacted to her as if he had been bewitched. The humming still soared throughout his body as he fought the urge to lie back down and take what he was craving. Kate.

Hawk walked over and tended to the fire. He needed something, anything to keep busy and stop his musing on Kate. He hoped she had been in the sleep daze as well and wouldn't remember what just took place. The quicker he got rid of this lass, the quicker he could focus on his life.

He hadn't felt his dragon in days, which left him edgy to begin with. It had to be that evil black smoke that hindered his dragon and left him human. Deep down he ached for his dragon, mourned him acutely. Nay, he still had to inhabit a dragon. If only there was a sign, a flinch, a growl, then he could dare to regain hope that his dragon still lived.

Hawk raked his hands through his red hair and hung his head as a vision of his sisters fleeing to the keep crept up on him. He closed his eyes, forcing himself to ease the memory away. He had to trust that MacGregor had taken them to safety. They had to be alive. Without his dragon or sisters he had nothing.

"I hope ye didnae mind." Kate yawned and stretched her arms to the sky.

He snapped his attention to her as she pulled a blanket around her shoulders. "Twas cold last night."

By the throbbing he felt betwixt his thighs, of course he didn't mind. In fact he liked it more than he should. "Ye should have woken me, I would have tended to the fire."

Hawk busied himself around camp, trying to forget about the way Kate had affected him. In addition, it looked like rain was approaching and, quite frankly, he welcomed it. Mayhap it would cool him for a while. "We need to make haste. Looks as if we might have a wet day ahead of us."

Kate stood and stretched then looked to the sky. "I'll only take a moment."

~

*W*alking a good distance from the campsite without wandering too far, Kate found the perfect bush to squat behind to relieve herself. Examining her surroundings until she felt safe, she hiked up her dress and squatted. She couldn't believe she had slept next to a man who wasn't her husband. It was improper, but her imagination of lurking creatures in the woods had gotten the best of her. She wouldn't dare tell Hawk she was too scared to sleep alone. He would no doubt laugh at her. Nay, it was much easier to blame the cold air.

Waking up in his arms had made her feel safe and alive all at the same time. His strength radiated from his body like a ray of sunlight, which only made her crave its warmth. Sexual instincts took over and her body had a mind of its own. Recalling the fiery trails he imprinted on her, a tingle set in the palm of her hand as she thought about running her fingers down the thick rigidness of his substantial chest. She yearned to feel his touch again.

Never having been with a man before, her body shouldn't have responded as it had. She didn't know the first thing about pleasing a man, yet by the way Hawk had nuzzled her skin, she knew he was a temptation. How careless had she been in trusting a complete stranger like this? If he so chose, he could take what he wanted from her and care naught about the consequences. God knew she was willing and that scared Kate more than ever.

Regardless of her attempts to open the door, he remained closed. What was it going to take to get through to him? And why should she care? If he didn't want to talk to her, mayhap it was for a good reason. Mayhap he didn't want her as a lover. Nay, she might be inexperienced and a wee bit naïve, but even through a sleep-filled fog, she'd felt his passion for her. She would just have to keep knocking until he answered.

Kate finished her business and walked toward the edge of a hill. In the distance she could see the mist lifting from a loch. Amazed at such beauty, she took in the view, wishing she had time to sketch in her journal. She envisioned herself sitting on a boulder, losing herself in nature's beauty. Thank goodness Sister Mary had found Kate's journal in the gardens and returned it to her. It would have been a heavy loss for Kate, for her passion was within those pages.

Walking closer to the cliff's edge for a better view, she escaped into the tranquility of the loch. The water rippled, cascading across the surface and disappearing as it reached the shore. She was unaware of the heavy approaching footsteps until Hawk stood next to her and cleared his throat. Startled, Kate lost her balance and her foot slipped off the cliff, sending dirt, mud, and her shoe raining down into the loch. She wobbled and her arms flailed as she tried to recapture her balance, when Hawk grabbed her by the waist and pulled her into his arms. "Ye shouldn't stand so close to the edge, Kate."

"And ye shouldn't sneak up on me like that." She slapped his chest and pushed away from him. "I told ye I would be back."

He gazed at his chest where she had hit him. "Aye, ye were taking too long. Ye see those graying clouds?" He pointed. "We'll be wet if we dinnae get moving."

Looking down over the cliff, Kate saw her shoe floating in the water. "By all that is holy! Now what am I supposed to do?"

"Och, lass, looks like ye'll need to go fishing." He smirked.

Kate glared at him. "'Tis no' the time to be jesting. Surely I can no' walk through the thick brush with bare feet. There are thistles everywhere."

Hawk placed his hands on his hips. "Well then, we have only one option here."

At this point Kate was more mortified for being a fool and standing too close to the cliff's edge. She wanted to be strong and show Hawk that indeed she had what it took to make it through the Highlands, but she was failing.

"And what might that be?"

He bent down in front of her and, in one fluid motion, picked her up over his shoulder.

"What are ye doing?" Kate yelled.

"We're getting oot of here before we get wet."

"This does not excuse ye for sneaking up on me."

"Ye can punish me later. Right now we need to make haste."

It was well into the noon hour when the sky opened up and cold rain fell all round them. Kate ducked her head under her cloak and squealed as she hide from the sudden rain. They had to find shelter somewhere, but where? They were deep in the Highlands. She waited patiently for Hawk to announce that they were stopping, but as if nothing ever affected him, he moved forward, following the trail as the rain rolled off his body.

After the shock of the cold rain wore off, Kate lifted the hood of her cloak. The rain slid down her head and dripped from the tips of her short brown hair. Looking up to the sky and squinting from the droplets pelting her eyes, Kate felt the wonder of the rain wash over her skin. She had never been outside in a storm before. Sure, she had run from it when not under the covered pathways at the abbey, but this was different.

Kate halted her mare and dismounted. She took off her dress, leaving her shift on. "Hawk, stop yer horse!" she called out through the rain. He didn't. "Hawk!" she called out again, louder. No response. She bent down and grabbed a handful of the muddiest dirt she could find and wadded it up into a big ball of dripping mess. Placing the mud ball in her right hand, she took aim and cocked her arm back. Before she had a chance to talk herself out of this mischievous deed, for she knew this could be a very bad decision, she let the mess of mud fly straight toward him.

The mud ball made its mark right in the center of the Hawk's back.

"Bloody Hell! What was that?" he shouted as he halted his horse and turned to look back at Kate. She stood laughing with muddy hands.

"I had to get yer attention some way. I want to stop." She chuckled.

Hawk twisted his tunic around to find a huge black splat mark dripping from it. "Lass," he grumbled, "ye'll pay for that." He removed his tunic and dismounted.

"I dinnae care." She threw her hands in the air. "Look at all this glorious rain." She spun around with her arms stretched out to the side.

~

*H*awk made his way to her, determined to make true his threat, but stopped abruptly. His anger quickly settled into amusement as he watched her. Mud soaked between her toes and splashed up on her legs as she danced innocently like a child in the rain. Her face was full of wonderment. Even though the sun wasn't shining today, her smile beamed like a ray of brightness, illuminating her face.

By the saints, she had taken off her dress and he could see right through the rain-soaked garment straight to her body, the same body that had been pressed against him only a few hours ago. Her wet shift stuck to her like a second skin, revealing her darkened peaks. His cock stiffened. Bloody Hell, she was beautiful.

Guilty for staring, he looked toward the forest as if she had no effect on him at all. It was wrong of him to stare; she was a lady. Having two sisters, he knew better. He would kill a man if he caught him looking at his sisters like he was staring at Kate.

Because temptation was wicked, he took in another view of Kate. He grinned as he bent down and picked up a handful of mud in his hands. He stood slowly savoring this moment, because after this, Kate would probably never speak to him again. If there was one lesson he had learned from his father, it was to never go back on your word, and he had threatened retaliation.

A moving target was hard to hit; timing was everything. Kate twirled to the right and Hawk let loose the mud ball, sending it flying straight to his target, hitting her in the chest. She stepped back from the sheer force of the mud and looked down at her chest. She glared at Hawk and sharply flung the mud from her shift. Aye, just as he had thought, the lass was surely going to give him a tongue-lashing. "I warned ye that ye would pay."

Kate bent down and picked up some more mud and gave him a mischievous grin. "Och, my laird, I do believe yer actions can no' be pardoned." And with that she threw another mud ball, hitting him in the face.

Hawk slung the mud from his face as he watched Kate laughing hysterically. The lass had gone too far. If she wanted a mud battle, well by God he was going to give it to her. Hastily he grabbed more mud, but this time he stalked toward her with long purposeful strides and she took off at a run.

It was much more difficult for Kate to run in the thick mud, plus Hawk outsized her by at least two people. He caught her around her waist. He thought it was quite amusing the way she kicked and fought him.

As he turned to place her on her feet, he tripped over an uprooted tree root, sending them both into a huge mud puddle. Hawk broke their fall by pulling Kate on top of him. The laughing stopped. Intently they locked eyes. Her breasts were wet through her shift and pressed against his hot skin. Water dripped from the ends of her hair and stuck to her face as she looked down at him. Gently, he reached up and tucked her wayward strands back behind her ear. Her cheekbones were high, her nose pert, and her lips were full, made to be thoroughly kissed. One taste was all he desired, and all he had to do was bring his lips to hers.

As if he had been doused with cold water, he found himself with a face full of mud. *Sneaky wench!* He was caught off guard. In one fluid motion he rolled Kate over onto her back and pinned her wrists above her head with one hand; in the other he held a fist of mud. Kate shook her head back and forth, but there was no stopping Hawk. He planted that handful of mud straight on her face and smeared it good. "Ye are one sneaky lass," he proclaimed. "Are ye going to stop with the mud, aye?"

She nodded.

"Good." Hawk released her wrist; however he couldn't will himself to release her body; the softness of her curves felt too damn good. He watched her wipe the mud from her face and was relieved to see her smiling.

"This was fun, Hawk. Ye should smile more often. Ye have a verra handsome smile." Kate took her hands and wiped the remaining mud from his face. He leaned his cheek into her touch and kissed her hand.

A bolt of lightning cracked through the sky and they both stilled. "'Tis best we find shelter for the night," he said as he looked to the sky.

As they made their way back to the soaked horses, the rain washed away most of the mud from their bodies, but their clothes remained dirty. As Kate approached her horse, Hawk threw his dirty tunic at her. Kate glared at him as if he had gone daft. "What's this?"

"Ye dirtied it. Ye wash it." Nonchalantly he mounted his horse and wrapped his plaid around his shoulders, then looked back to Kate still standing by her horse with her mouth open, stunned.

With her hands on her hips she replied, "I'm no' washing it." She wadded the material into a ball and set it on her saddle as she put her dress on, then mounted her horse.

Hawk shook his head. "Ye have much to learn, lass." And if he was completely honest with himself, he wanted to be the one who taught her the ways of pleasing a man. He didn't know when it had happened, but the lass had crawled under his skin and straight to his heart. On the other hand, he knew better than to think of Kate in that light. It wouldn't be an easy task to let her go; but alas, he had to.

12

The storm was unyielding. Gusty winds blew in from the east, rolling thunder crashed all around them as lightning cracked the sky. For what seemed like an eternity Hawk searched for some kind of shelter while they made their way through the soggy Highlands. There was nothing. They were tired and hungry and he was afraid Kate would catch her death out here, for she was shivering from the cold rain.

Forging ahead, determined to find shelter, Hawk squinted through the sheets of rain in front of him. A flicker of light from down in the valley caught his attention. Aye, they were close. Nestled between two enormous hills, a village came into view. Hawk knew the area well; they were right outside of Helmfirth's border.

"Kate!" Hawk yelled behind him. "There's a village ahead. We'll have shelter soon."

If Kate answered he couldn't hear over the heavy rain. Taking a glance over his shoulder, he was relieved to see that she still followed faithfully behind.

As Hawk approached the end of the trail they had been following, there was a slight decline in the terrain, enough that he knew Kate wouldn't make it downhill without help. It was steep and, if they approached the wrong way, they could end up sliding down the hill, causing a mudslide.

Kate caught up with him and halted her horse next to his. Through chattering teeth, she asked, "I suppose ye're going to tell me we're going down that hill?"

Hawk hopped down off his horse and took a closer look at the slope. Indeed it was going to be a rigorous task. Large boulders dotted the area, which alarmed him. One false move and they would most definitely slide down the slippery slope and possibly to their death.

Hawk strode through the mud over to Kate. "Ye're riding with me." He scooped her up into his arms and placed her on his horse.

"But what aboot me horse?"

"Dinnae fash yerself, she'll make it. 'Tis ye I worry aboot."

Without another word Hawk mounted his horse, placing Kate in front of him. He felt her nestle into his warmth and he wished he had more to give her to keep warm. He grabbed the reins and bent his head down to her ear, whispering, "Do ye trust me, Kate?"

She nodded and gripped his forearms for dear life.

Slippery step by slippery step they carefully descended, trying to avoid their deaths. The steed's hooves slid and wobbled like a newly born fawn, yet the horse stood true, regaining its balance. "Easy does it, laddie," Hawk reassured his horse. He could feel the tension in Kate's shivering body. Her nails were digging half-moon trenches in his arms as she held on to him with all her might. "We're almost there, lass."

When the last hoof reached solid ground, the tautness in Kate's body relaxed. She leaned her head back and rested it on Hawk's chest. "I've never been so close to death in all me life."

"Death? Och, I thought ye said ye trusted me," Hawk teased.

"I do, but ye can no' tempt fate like that."

"Fate?" Hawk puffed out his chest. "Nay, I'm a skilled Highlander and dinnae ye forget it. We've made it thus far and surely it wasn't oot of luck."

Kate giggled as he continued toward the village, for they were mere minutes away from shelter and food.

"Wait." Kate looked over her shoulder toward the top of the slope where her horse stood. "What aboot Ninny? We can no' leave her oot here like this."

"She'll catch up. We need to get ye oot of this rain. Ye're going to catch yer death if we stay oot here any longer." Hawk kicked his horse into a canter as they sped through the valley and headed straight to the flickering light.

Smoke billowed from the tavern's thatch roof, a warm glow from the inside beckoned an inviting welcome, and the aroma of stew made his stomach growl. Hawk helped Kate dismount and they hastily walked inside the tavern. With the storm raging outside, he was surprised to see a few patrons still lingering, laughing, and drinking the night away.

As soon as the barkeep saw them, she glared, scrutinizing the two. "What brings ye oot in this weather?" The keeper wiped her hands on her apron.

Hawk cleared his throat. "We got caught in the rainstorm and need a place to stay—for the night."

"Looks like ye need more than a place to sleep, laddie." The keeper ran her eyes over Kate's soaking wet clothes down to her dirty feet.

Hawk looked at Kate. The lass was shaking so hard he could hear her teeth chatter. He had to get her out of those wet clothes before she got sick. "Miss, as ye can see, we need yer help. We mean ye no trouble."

"Aye, laddie, I have one room available that should be right nice for ye and yer wife." The keeper crossed her arms over her plump chest. "The mistress is yer wife, aye? I will no' have ye living in sin under me roof."

Hawk swallowed hard and looked over at Kate shaking. He would go so far as to tell the woman that dragons existed if it meant getting Kate warm. "Aye."

Wide-eyed, Kate looked at him as if he had grown two heads. Hawk shrugged his shoulders and nodded toward the keeper as if telling her to play along.

"Aye, in fact we just got married. We were oot for a romantic horse ride when the rain caught up with us." Kate gave her best attempt at a smile.

The keeper smiled back. "Well, lass, since ye're newlywed, I'll see to it that ye both are taken care of." She poked her head behind a wall that separated the bar from the rooms and shouted down the hallway to her daughter. "Eva, ready the room down the hall, aye." The keeper looked back at Kate, eyeing her up and down. "And fetch one of your dresses." The keeper looked further down to Kate's dirty bare feet. "And shoes."

A small tub sitting in front of the hearth was the first thing that caught Hawk's attention when he opened the door to the bedchamber. "Kate, ye need to get oot of those wet clothes and into a hot bath." He walked her to the tub and she began to undress as if she was the only one in the room. Hawk reached out his hand but paused before he touched her. What was he thinking? He had no claim over her, she could manage undressing by herself. "I'll give ye privacy. I'll be downstairs."

Quickly, Kate put her hands over her breasts. "Dinnae ye need a bath too? Ye should get oot of yer wet clothes."

"Nay, ye go ahead. I'll make do." Before he changed his mind he quit the room.

The door shut behind him and Hawk scrubbed his hands down his face, trying to erase the image of Kate, naked in the tub. God's blood he wanted to stay and wash her hair, wash her beautiful body. The need of wanting to take care of her took him by surprise.

He turned back to the door and placed his hand on the latch. Damn himself for a fool, he was going back in. As he began to open the door he heard a click; Kate had locked it. Hawk rested his forehead on the door and closed his eyes. *Thank the Gods that be.*

Taking a moment to settle his lustful urges, he pushed off the door and strode down the corridor to the bar to fetch food for Kate and quench his thirst for mead. He would need a lot of it to rid his mind of Kate.

Taking a chair at the bar, Hawk sat brooding, heavily in thought.

The keeper's husband tended to the bar patrons, and placed a tankard of mead in front of Hawk. "Looks as if ye'll be needing a few more of these before the night ends."

Hawk nodded and drained his tankard. "Aye."

Indeed he would. It took all his resolve to leave Kate when what he craved to do was bathe in the tub with her. To feel her wet skin next to his, to feel the fullness of her breasts, to kiss her long slender neck, to feel his cock deep inside her. Aye, it was a good thing that his arse had left that room as quick as wildfire.

It was becoming more and more difficult to shut the lass out. She had a way with him like no other; she made him smile. Her innocence amused him. By the way she looked at him, he knew all he had to do was make the first move and take what he wanted. Hell, mayhap he should do just that. Bed the lass and get her out of his system. Let lust take over. It wasn't as if Kate was going to stay at Helmfirth; he'd promised to take her to Black Stone. So why not take what he was yearning for, then let the lass go?

Besides, even if he wanted to be the proper gentleman, she wouldn't want to stay with him. With the uncertainty at Helmfirth, his sisters, and his dragon, he couldn't possibly bring her into his world. He had nothing to give. And if, nay—when his dragon did rear its beastie head, Kate would never understand. Being as innocent as she was and having led such a sheltered life up to this point, throwing a dragon into her world might drive her off the edge.

Nay, he wouldn't be responsible for that. Kate had left the abbey to find herself, not get caught up with the likes of him. He would only break her heart. In fact, because of who he was, he never allowed himself the pleasures of a lass. But when Kate was around, pure raw male instincts coursed through his body, urging him to claim her. *Make her mine.*

Hawk furrowed his brows as he finished another tankard of mead. As he saw it, he only had two choices here. Whichever he chose would define him for the rest of his long immortal life. Be the bastard his cock wanted him to be; claim the lass and let her go. Or be the man his father would be proud of and make an honest woman out of

Kate. Make her his wife, start a family, and live happily ever after. For a moment he dared to dream.

The rain pelted down on the thatch roof and dragged Hawk's attention to the storm raging outside. He knew he had to make a choice now. So which man was he going to be?

"Here ya go, laddie." The man from behind the bar set a tray of provisions out for him to take to Kate.

Taking another pull from a fresh tankard, Hawk nodded his thanks. As soon as his feet hit the ground, his head spun and he grabbed a nearby chair to catch his balance.

The keeper's husband smirked at his distress as if it wasn't the first time he had seen a man intoxicated from his mead.

Hawk smiled at the man. "The mead is strong, aye?"

"I make it meself. An auld family recipe," the man said proudly.

"I thank ye for yer hospitality." Carefully Hawk quit the bar and headed back to the corridor. With blurred vision, he found the room and slammed his fist against the door, knocking loudly. "Kate! 'Tis me," he slurred.

The door opened and his breath escaped him. Her heather scent engulfed him, their eyes locked and suddenly the air between them turned hot. He couldn't stop eyeing her. He hadn't been gone long, yet it felt like he hadn't seen her in years.

"What took ye so long? I was worried," Kate asked.

He came to his senses and staggered past her. "Here's some fresh bread and stew." He placed the tray on a table, then sat heavily on the bed, pulling his boots off.

Sitting down at the table, Kate took in the aroma of the stew. "This smells divine." She drew the spoon up to her mouth and blew while Hawk watched her. "And it tastes even better."

Hawk growled. He knew exactly where he wanted that mouth of hers—on his skin.

Kate looked at him and paused before she took another spoonful of stew. She cleared her throat. "Eva has freshened up the tub for ye."

What was he doing? He couldn't stop staring at her. If she licked her lips one more time, it would break him.

"Hawk, what's wrong? Ye're frightening me." She flew out of her chair and strode over to him.

He grabbed her shift at the waist and pulled her close, resting his head on her breasts. He nuzzled into her softness and took in a deep breath. "Ye should stay away from me, Kate."

He felt her fingers gently run through his hair. Kate looked down at him and cupped his face. "But I dinnae want to." She slipped her hands behind his neck, pulling him closer and pressed her lips slowly to his. Christ, her lips were as soft and divine as he'd imagined.

Hawk relished the moment, allowing himself to be completely swept away by this beautiful lass. She softly caressed his skin, leaving gooseflesh behind. Drawing back slowly she broke the kiss, yet she lingered only a breath away from his lips.

Holding nothing back, he wrapped his arms around her and brought her to his lap. Primal instincts pushed him forward as he captured her lips once more. He held her head in the palms of his hands as he slipped his tongue past her lips. Willingly she opened for him, allowing him to take what he wanted, what he craved. Surprised that she didn't stop him, he continued to deepen the kiss feverishly.

Gripping his hands in the bed linens, he fought the urge to rip Kate's shift off. Something stirred deep within his core...something raw...something erotic...commanding him to claim her. A familiar guttural growl vibrated through his body and he knew he had to stop before it was too late.

Hawk pulled back, breaking their connection. Kate opened her eyes and he'd never seen anything so beautiful in his life. He traced his finger over her red, kissed-swollen lips. Her cheeks were flushed and her breathing labored. She looked up at him with lust-hooded eyes. She wanted more, but he wasn't sure he could give more.

"I'm going to take a bath." He placed her on her feet as he stood. Unwrapping his kilt, he headed toward the tub. He didn't dare look back at her, for he had made his decision and he didn't need her to change his mind. He was going to be an honorable man and leave the lass alone. He called over his shoulder to her, "Get some sleep."

~

*I*rritated, Kate flung the furs off. She had been tossing and turning most of the night. In-between pretending to sleep, she'd watched Hawk secretly as he finished his bath and prepared a place to sleep on the floor. She had wished that he would slip into bed with her. Being close to him made her feel protected, safe. When he wasn't beside her she missed him.

How was she ever going to break through to him? She wasn't daft; he wanted her as much as she wanted him, yet he was holding back. *"Ye should stay away from me, Kate."* But why? Why did he want her to stay away? *There was an attack on his village, perhaps someone is after him.*

Mayhap it was because she was naïve, innocent in the ways of life and love. It wasn't as though she had ever been in love with a man before, especially a Highlander. Definitely her situation wasn't the proper way for a lass to find love, yet it was exactly the way she had imagined love would feel. She couldn't understand the fluttering butterflies that she felt when Hawk walked into a room, or the way her heart skipped a beat. His eyes looked right through her into her soul.

Rolling over on her side, Kate huffed. Nay, this couldn't be love. It had to be lust. Some kind of bewitchment. Sister Mary had warned her about love and lust and its wicked temptations. Thinking nothing of it back then, now she wished she had paid more attention to Mary's words of wisdom. She needed to keep her virtue pure.

Flipping over on her back, Kate stared at the ceiling for what seemed like forever. Soft snoring came from the floor, constantly reminding her she wasn't alone. *Why does it have to be so blessed hot in here?*

Annoyed with her inner musings, Kate got out of bed to find her satchel, hoping the rain hadn't soaked her things. Careful not to wake Hawk, she searched for her quill, ink, and journal quietly. Thank God that the fire in the hearth was still lit and burning bright. She had missed not being able to draw since she left the abbey and with a restless night ahead of her, she needed something to pass the time.

Snoring from the floor brought Kate's attention to Hawk as he lay in peaceful slumber. She smiled and took in his true beauty. Aye, she knew exactly what she wanted to draw. Grabbing her supplies, she sat down beside him, marveling at the Highlander. He lay on his back with one hand behind his head. His face soft, yet stern. His jawline, strong. He was every bit a man. Nay, he was more than that, she thought as she began to sketch out his facial features.

She paused for a moment and absorbed more of him as her eyes traveled to his naked chest. Deep brown freckles dappled the muscled expanse. She had never seen so many muscles. Taken away by the moment, she reached out and caressed his chest right where she knew his heart lay. Even though he begged to differ, she knew there was a heart in there somewhere.

Her fingers traced further down the ridges of endless muscle until she reached a trail of fine red hair disappearing under the fur. Hawk moaned and Kate's eyes went wide, stopping her sweet assault on his skin. *By the saints, Kate! Keep yer hands to yerself!*

He settled back to sleep and she blew out a breath she hadn't realized she'd been holding. As she continued to look farther down his body, the fur bulged between his legs and it struck her then how much her touch affected the Highlander. She might be innocent but there was no mistaking that Hawk wanted her. She hadn't realized how one touch could hold so much power. What would have happened if she hadn't stopped? Being a virgin, was she ready to explore all the wicked temptations Sister Mary had warned her about? Aye, if it involved Hawk then most definitely she wanted to explore.

Returning to her sketch before she found herself in trouble, Kate drew the night away until she could no longer keep her eyes open. Curling up next to Hawk, she found her peace and drifted off to sleep.

13

*L*ike a gust of wind, two menacing men in cloaks strode into the tavern. The barkeeper raised his eyebrows, placed his hands on the bar and leaned toward them. "The bar is closed."

With an abundance of charm and confidence one of the men took a seat in front of the barkeep.

"I want no trouble here," the barkeeper warned.

"Relax, auld man. There will be no trouble as long as ye tell me what I want to know."

The other man joined in and sat next to his companion sheepishly. "Aye, what master wants, master gets."

"And what may it be ye want?" the barkeep asked as he poured the two men tankards of mead. "We have verra little coin and our rooms are full. All I can offer ye is a wee bit of mead."

One man drank from the tankard then set it down, swallowing the liquid slowly. "I do no' want yer coin, nor a room. I need to know if ye've seen a particular lass here in the last day or so."

The barkeep laughed. "We see a lot of lasses around here."

The man removed his hood and ice blue eyes pinned the barkeep as if he found his laughter appalling. He gripped his hands around the tankard until his knuckles whitened. Being secluded in the ice cave for months had left the man irritable and his hatred festered like an infected wound.

His frustration showed through as the tankard in his hand froze and cracked with ice. "The lass may be traveling with a Highlander."

With his nose turned up, the man's companion sniffed the air long and deep. "Aye, master, I can smell the dragon."

Taking a step back, the barkeep stuttered, "I...I think ye should leave."

The man with the icy stare reached up and grabbed the man's head and slammed it down on the bar, holding it there while he whispered in his ear, "Where is the lass?"

"I...swear...I do no' know who ye be talking aboot!" the barkeep cried out.

Just then the barkeep heard his wife's heavy footsteps coming from the corridor. "Husband, are ye done cleaning?" She rounded the corner and gasped as she watched her husband struggling against the stranger's hold. "Have mercy, sir, please," she screamed and ran to her husband, but didn't reach him in time. From out of nowhere ice crystals flew from the man's hand, covering the woman. An ice sickle as sharp as a dirk pierced her chest. Cracking ice echoed in the empty tavern as the freeze rapidly consumed the woman's body. Stunned, she looked down at her chest, terrified as she saw the ice creep up her body. At once the woman fell to the ground, shattering into a million pieces.

The man with the icy touch exhaled, blowing out a puff of frigid air. "Now, auld man, are ye going to tell where the lass is?"

～

A crash thumped through Hawk's hung-over state, startling him from sleep. "Bloody Hell." He looked over to find Kate once again snuggled next to him. Her eyelashes rested on her plump cheeks, her lips parted slightly; she was a true beauty. Reaching down, he brushed away a lock of brown hair from her face, then noticed a black smudge marring her cheek. What had she been up to?

As he wiped away the smudge he found a quill in her hand and her journal next to her. Knowing it was an invasion of her privacy, he nevertheless took the journal and began to close it when he saw her drawings. He flipped through the pages and stopped when he reached a recognizable image. God's teeth! It was him, sleeping. Every stroke of the quill was perfection. Every freckle was in the right place.

As he flipped through the pages he found himself enthralled by the breathtaking sketches of birds, flowers of many shapes, and animals. She had brought out nature's true beauty with accurate details. The feathers burst from a page as if the bird flew out of the parchment. On another page, he traced a drawing of a flower in bloom and swore he could feel its true texture and smell its sweet fragrance.

He looked back down at Kate, to see her staring at him. "Ye know 'tis rude to look through folks personal belongings."

"I know, but Kate, ye have a true talent here." He closed the journal and handed it to her.

"So did ye like it?" She sat up and took the journal, holding it to her chest.

"Like what?" He knew of what she was asking, but pretended that he hadn't seen the portrait.

Kate huffed. "Yer drawing, silly."

Hawk stood and stretched as he fought off the remainder of last night's mead. Cold air licked his skin as the fur fell to the ground. Shite! He was naked. Turning three shades of red, he looked at her as she cleared her throat and grinned into her lap. Without looking, she grabbed the fur and handed it to Hawk, who was too mortified to move.

A crash from down the corridor startled him. "Kate, get dressed."

This time the crash sounded close and every fiber in his body told him to be on alert. His skin rippled as he felt the sensation to shift.

His mind was telling him to do so, yet his body refused the message. Hawk pulled up his trews. "I'll be right back."

"Wait! Hawk, what's going on?" Kate stood and searched for her dress. "I'll go with ye."

"Nay, ye stay here. And be ready to leave when I get back." As he left the room, he slipped on his tunic and proceeded with caution down the corridor.

With each sobering step he took the urgency to fight elevated to alarming heights. With no weapons, how was he going to defend himself if the opportunity arose? Hawk paused before he rounded the corner to the bar. Cracking his neck from side to side, he closed his eyes and reached down deep inside to call forth his dragon. He balled his fists as a shot of pain pinned his chest right where the wyvern had bitten him. Bloody Hell! Hawk doubled over in agony as he clutched his stomach. A growl rumbled inside him, sending out a warning sign. Skin rippled and sweat poured from his pores; all the while his body acted as if it was fighting off an enemy from deep within. As if his dragon was fighting the black smoke.

After what seemed like forever, Hawk's eyes flipped open and swirled with rage. Another Dragonkine was here. He could feel it. Taking in a deep breath and keeping his back pressed against the wall, Hawk peeked around the corner and saw a cloaked man manhandling the barkeep. As he looked to the other man, his blood boiled. It was him, the thief, the wyvern.

Hawk raged inside. The thief was going to die.

Hawk took one step away from the wall then paused. "Kate." If something happened to him she would be left alone. Hawk stepped back into the shadows. As he waited for his temper to recede, he could hear the sobbing barkeep pleading for his life.

"Please, have mercy, I will tell ye what ye want to know. Last night...a lass and a verra brawny Highlander came into the tavern, late. They asked for a room, and that be all I know."

The man grinned evilly and patted his prisoner on the head. "Where is the room?"

The barkeep pointed toward the corridor. "Down there...to the left."

The man let go of his hold and nodded to his companion as he strode toward the corridor to the grunting sound of a man's throat being sliced.

~

"Where is it?" Kate frantically searched for her amulet. What possessed her to take it off in the first place she would never understand. Never once had she taken it off, yet last night she had. She couldn't explain it, but her necklace made her feel safe, as secure as if her mother still watched over her. She knew it to be silly, yet she found comfort in that jewel.

Throwing furs left and right, she became more and more frustrated with herself. Hawk would be back soon and she had to be ready to go. "Hawk?" Kate stood straight up, stunned. Hawk was in trouble. She could feel his distress as if he was inside her. Her arms tingled and itched as she glanced at them. A glow trailed and swirled up and down her arms all the way down to her hands. Power surged through the paths, leaving behind something she could only describe as magic. "By the saints!" Bewildered, she rubbed her arms.

A white mist floated up from the floor. Desperately she tried to avoid the fog as it encircled her body, but it was of no use. The thick white smoke swirled up, encasing her in magic.

The door swung open and Hawk rushed in and abruptly halted. "Kate?" He couldn't believe what he saw. A cloud of white magic swirled around her, engulfing her. Hawk reached out to grab her hand and the whiteness burned his palm. "God's bones! This can no' be. Ye're a Drag..."

At exactly that moment, the two men from the bar skidded to a halt right outside the bedchamber door as soon as they saw Kate. Hawk's eyes swirled and his claws were out as he stood in a protective stance in front of her. He growled low and deep, sending out a fierce warning.

The man with the cold blue stare reached out and touched the wall behind him and Hawk watched it turn to solid ice. The man continued, walking the perimeter of the room, never taking his hand off the wall. A layer of ice replaced the once mortar and stone, creating a prison of ice around them. What struck Hawk as odd was the evil way he looked at Kate.

"Who are ye?" Hawk asked.

"It does no' matter who I am. Ye should be more worried aboot what I'm going to do to ye. Ye should have stayed dead," the man hissed.

His companion laughed sinisterly as black smoke billowed around him.

Hawk looked from the ice man to the smoke man, sizing each one up. It was a standoff. Who was going to make the first move?

The white mist faded as Kate came to. Unexplainable power surged through her, swirling trails on her arms and chest. Something deep inside told her these men were here to hurt Hawk, but why, she did not know. She could feel the power intensifying in the room as the man in front of Hawk controlled a ring of black smoke in his hands, when from the corner of her eye she saw an ice sickle flying through the air, aimed right for Hawk. Without hesitation, Kate darted in front of him and placed her hands out in front of her, closing her eyes tightly. White light connected with the ice sickle, shattering it into falling shards. Then she switched her sights on the man chilling the room and blasted him with her light, sending him flying backwards out into the corridor. As if it was second nature to her, she spun around and blasted the man with the black magic twice, sending him straight on his arse, knocked out cold. She had moved so quickly she had caught the men off guard.

She faced Hawk with her hands still in front of her and he ducked. "Kate's 'tis me, Hawk."

The smoke cleared as the tension in the bedchamber faded. Kate, still in shock, glanced at the palms of her hands as she felt the magic settle on her skin. She shook her head. "I dinnae understand."

Hawk approached her. "Remind me to never anger ye." He smirked.

She looked at him and back down at her hands. "I—"

Hawk cupped her face. "We'll figure this oot, lass. But right now we need to get oot of here."

"Aye."

Hawk grabbed her hand and led her to the giant hole in the wall where the door once stood. Then she noticed her amulet glowing under the bed. "Wait." She pulled away from Hawk, grabbed the necklace and put it on. Every last tingle, itch, and power left her body as if it had been lifted from her. Kate shook her head. *What's happening to me?*

"Kate, we have to go."

14

"We need to talk," Magnus said as he halted his horse and dismounted. "We'll camp here tonight." The cave was dark and small, barely big enough for two people. The rain had been relentless and fatigue set in as they tore through the Highlands, hunting down their daughter's scent. She was close; he could feel it.

The forest was saturated by the recent rainfall. Magnus was lucky to find a few pieces of dry wood. He dumped the wood just inside the cave, bent down and puffed out his cheeks, then blew. In no time, flames began to kindle the logs and a fire roared to life.

Magnus stood and was hit in the chest with a sudden thump against his ribcage. There she was sitting on the other side of the flames, as beautiful as the first day he had seen her twenty-and-six years ago. Long brown hair cascaded down her shoulders and stopped at her slender waist. Deep hazel eyes held the kind of innocence of a child, free of sin. A dragon never forgets that kind of beauty.

Though the woman was mesmerizing, Magnus was still quite infuriated with her, and she had a lot of explaining to do. Although he possessed a gentle patience, he wanted to shake every last answer out of her. He would tread softly and rein in his rage if he wanted answers.

All these years he'd had a daughter he knew nothing about. Glaring at the woman as if he could see straight through her, he paused and wondered what his daughter looked like. Did she have her mother's hair and big, alluring eyes? Did she have the same flaw-less, pale creamy skin? Christ, he hoped she did, for his rugged features would look hideous on a young lass.

"Come sit, Magnus," The Dragonkine female patted the spot next to her and handed him a piece of stale bread.

Magnus took the bread and popped it in his mouth. "I'll stand," he said as he crossed his arms over his chest.

"I'm truly sorry for hurting ye, but ye must know everything I did was to protect our daughter."

"Even keeping her away from her da? Fia, if that is indeed yer name, I could have protected the both of ye."

"Aye, Fia is my true name. As I said, I did everything in my power to protect her."

"Then tell me, tell me why. Why didnae ye come to me?"

"I couldn't, Magnus. That night at the tavern, I wasn't supposed to be there, nor in yer realm. I was bored back home and I let curiosity guide me. That's when I decided to break the rules and leave the females and come here. But what I didn't expect was meeting ye." Fia looked intensely into the flickering flames. "Ye're verra handsome. I had never met a man like ye before and I knew what ye were as soon as I set eyes on ye."

Magnus stiffened and worked the tension from his jaw. He didn't need Fia trying to soften his rough edges; he wanted answers.

Fia continued. "After I found oot I was pregnant, I got scared. I couldn't return to my realm, Mistress wouldn't be pleased. Leaving the females in the first place was bad enough, not to mention me being pregnant." She hung her head in shame. "I couldn't go back."

"Why didn't ye tell me?"

"I tried. I went back to the tavern a few times, but never saw ye. Then the next thing I knew the babe came and I was running for our lives. We hid in small villages until the death dragons came close to us. We were always one step ahead of them, until one day I realized our daughter needed a better life. That's when I took her to Dunfermline Abbey. She was safe there and I was never far away."

"Ye hid her away without once thinking how I would feel aboot it. Do ye no' believe a father should know that he has a child? Christ, Fia, ye were being chased by death!" As Fia's story went on, Magnus became more and more hurt by her actions. It saddened him no end that he couldn't be there to protect his family. A family he'd had no idea existed.

Fia's cheeks reddened. "I did what I thought was right!"

"Och, but look where yer plan has led our daughter. Now she's in danger." He glared at her. "Ye call that doing right? And who was going to explain to her about her powers? She is a Dragonkine female, aye?"

Fia crossed her arms over her chest, shutting Magnus out. "Aye," she bit back.

"She doesn't even know how to mask her scent. Did ye think aboot that?"

"They would have never found her if she had stayed at the abbey."Fia sniffled.

There was a long pause as Magnus tamped down his anger. Being a man who was led by his emotions, it was difficult for him to maintain his composure. He had been stewing ever since Fia had come to him back at Black Stone seeking his help.

"I put a spell on an amulet that would hide her powers and her markings as long as she wore it. The amulet has your blood in it to protect her."

"You did what?"

"I...I"

Magnus stood in front of Fia. "Because that amulet contains pure dragon blood. Ye've put our daughter in danger. The Creepers ye've been running from are part of an army that want to awaken Drest. That blood around her neck will lead them straight to her."

Fia stood in shock. "I didnae know."

Magnus closed his eyes tightly, irritated by the woman's lack of trust in him. He was a Highlander of honor, as loyal as they come. The fact that Fia hadn't trusted him was like a thorn twisting in his side, festering the more he learned. If she had come to him sooner, he could have protected them both without some spell, and his daughter would be safe.

"Magnus." Fia went to him, unlacing the top of her dress. "Look at me." He opened his eyes and stood speechless at the red swirling markings on her chest. Fia grabbed his hand and placed it on her mate markings. "No matter how angry ye be wit' me, ye can no' turn me away. I am yer mate."

Glaring at the markings, Magnus knew it to be true. All Dragonkine females were born with shimmering-iridescent, Celtic swirls up and down their arms and chest. But once mated, the female's markings would turn the color of their mate's dragon.

Magnus's heart was beating so fast he thought it would beat right out of his chest. His dragon paced inside as he waited for him to accept his mate. Looking from her hand to her flawless face, Magnus shook his head. "Ye may be me mate, but I dinnae have to accept ye, Fia." He strode past her, leaving her bewildered. He made his way to the front of the cave and sat with his back to her as he watched out over the blackness of the night. The forest was quiet. The stars were bright against the black sky.

How quickly had his life turned from gray to black? It had been enough to battle Marcus and the Creepers, and death. Knowing he had a daughter who was now in danger prevailed above all other thoughts. A shiver raced down his spine and he pulled his cloak tighter around his shoulders. He knew he had been harsh on the woman, but she had hurt his pride, and forgiveness would come with a cost.

He leaned his ample body against the cave wall and crossed his arms over his chest. His red, long hair slightly blew in the gentle night breeze as he drifted further into his thoughts until the early morn.

Somewhere between early morn and the sun peeking behind the

clouds, a sudden blast of power struck him. His body tensed; it was her, his daughter. He could feel her as if she ran through his veins. Magnus stood and was struck again. "Kate," he called out.

Fia had been awake pacing the back of the cave most of the night. Pausing, she spun around to face Magnus. "I feel it too."

"I know where she is; it's time to go." Magnus fetched his horse while Fia kicked sand over the fire to put it out. She collected the furs from the ground, then quickly ran outside the cave slamming smack into Magnus. "I pray that we are no' too late. If anything happens to Kate—"

Magnus grabbed hold of Fia's arms and held her frightened stare. "I will hunt down the bastards and kill them wit' me own bare hands," Magnus seethed. "Besides I feel her power, no danger. But we must leave now while I can still feel her."

With that, they both the horse and rode hard through the forest and down a hill. They came upon a tavern in the valley.

As they approached the village, gray smoke billowed from the tavern that now lay in a smoldering heap.

"Nay!" Fia jumped from the horse and ran to the charred building. She fell to her knees, sobbing. "Nay!"

Magnus dismounted and stood over the gray rubble on the ground. Bending down, he scooped up some ash and held it in his hand, allowing it to pour between his fingers. His daughter could not be dead; he would not accept it. He had felt her moments ago.

As if he had been struck by lightning, a jolt shook him to the core. "Aye, Kate."

"Ye can feel her?" Fia slowly stood.

"Aye, she was here."

"But she's no' here now." Fia looked around the village. "Where could she have gone?"

Magnus retrieved his horse and mounted. "My guess, she's in Helmfirth."

Reaching out to Fia, he helped her mount the horse. "How do ye know she would go to Helmfirth?" she inquired.

The warrior positioned Fia in front of him and gripped the reins.

"Helmfirth is no' quite a march from here. If she was farther away, I dinnae think I would still be able to feel her."

"I hope ye are right. I can no' feel her."

Magnus sternly regarded Fia. "Dinnae doubt me, woman. I am dragon." And with a click of his tongue, he pushed his charger into a gallop. He was going to find his daughter alive. He swore it.

15

*A*s they approached Helmfirth, Hawk's mind raced with images of his village in flames, in complete ruin, and he wondered what might still remain. A few details of that tragic day were still blurry at best. There were two images he couldn't shake: his sisters and his hawks. If any harm had come to Lana and Gwen he would never forgive himself.

A slight shifting movement in front of him brought his attention to Kate. On horseback, she had sat in front of him silently since they left the tavern. He wanted to ask her so many questions, but thought better of it. It was bluntly apparent she did not want to talk about what had happened back in the bedchamber. When Hawk felt her magic he knew what she was and was surprised he hadn't felt it sooner. Then again, his dragon had been gone.

As they reached the village, an acrid smell of burning earth and flesh brought his fears to reality as he saw Helmfirth in ruins. Forthwith Hawk halted his horse and dismounted. In shock, he took in the wrecked village. Charred, decaying bodies littered the marketplace, carts that were once full of vegetables had been smashed to pieces, and smoke still smoldered from where once had stood the butcher's shop.

A gray and black striped feather floated down from the heavens and landed on the ground in front of him. He bent down and picked it up; the ends were singed. As much as he didn't want to face the sickening feeling gnawing at his gut, he needed to know what remained of his hawks. *Arlen!*

Taking off at full speed, he passed the village market and straight through to the glen, praying to the gods that be that his raptors were still alive. Jumping over a few fallen tree branches, he reached the hut. Hawk skidded to a stop. Feathers swirled and lay in a heap where his mew had once stood. Scorched iron cages were left behind, telling a horrid tale that his raptors had suffered a great deal. Hawk looked up to the skies and called out to Arlen, hoping he had fled the massacre. He spun around, desperately searching for some small sign that his goshawk or, for that matter, any of his quarry had made it out before the flames engulfed them.

After a moment of silence, Hawk fell to his knees with his head hung in defeat. If his mew had fallen to the attack, then there wasn't much hope for the keep. Slumped over with his head in his hands, he couldn't will himself to check the keep for his sisters. He couldn't bear the pain of seeing Lana and Gwen dead. There was too much death to bear.

A warm hand touched his shoulder and brought him comfort as his body shook uncontrollably. He looked up to see Kate gazing down at him sorrowfully. He grabbed her by the waist and pulled her into his embrace, wrapping his arms around her tightly. He needed her warmth, her touch to take the pain away. His body fell into hers as she ran her fingers through his hair. She was his calmness, his still waters. Without saying a word, he felt her sympathy for him in every touch. He took the comfort she offered.

"Hawk, 'tis really ye!" A familiar voice broke through the silence.

He didn't dare to believe his ears, however he looked towards the glen where the voice came from, praying it be true. He cleared the lump from his throat and blinked his vision clear. "Lana?" Hawk stood, stunned to see his sister. "Ye be alive?"

Running into her brother's arms, Lana cried uncontrollably. "Aye, I thought ye were dead."

Squeezing her as tight as he could without breaking her, Hawk spun his sister around then placed her on her feet. "Where's—"

At that moment, Gwen came running, huffing and puffing as she reached her sister and brother. "Och, Lana, ye run too fast."

Hawk smiled and strode over to his younger sister and hugged her. "Ye dinnae understand how happy I am that ye be well."

"Of course I am. 'Tis ye that gave us a scare." Gwen said sternly and hit him in the stomach.

Lana grabbed Hawk's arm and pulled him toward the keep. "I'm sure ye must be hungry. And MacGregor will be pleased to see that our Laird of Helmfirth has returned. Not to mention wee Duncan. He's missed his Uncle Hawk."

"Aye, and ye should meet the tall, dark stranger that chased the beastie away," Gwen informed him with a grin from ear to ear.

"A stranger? Ye allowed a stranger to stay inside the keep?" Hawk grumbled.

"Aye, MacGregor keeps a keen eye on him." Lana winked at Gwen.

With Lana on one arm and Gwen on the other, Hawk looked back to find Kate following behind. How could he have been so rude? "Wait. I want to introduce ye to Kate. Lana and Gwen, this is Kate. Kate, these are me sisters."

"'Tis a pleasure to meet ye both." Kate nodded and smiled.

The sisters looked at her, stunned. It wasn't every day that Hawk brought home a lass. In fact he had never brought one home. Lana looked from Hawk then at Kate. "Och, welcome to our home, Kate." She pulled her into a warm inviting hug.

Then Gwen stepped in. "Welcome, Kate. If ye need anything let me know." Gwen took Kate's hands in hers and looked her up and down. "Ye look like the same size as me. I'll bring ye some clean dresses."

Kate bashfully smiled and tucked a lock of hair behind her ear. "Thank ye."

~

*K*ate could only imagine what Hawk's sisters thought of her. By the way her body ached, she knew her face had given away just how tired she was. Embarrassment flooded her when she looked down at her dirty clothes. Quickly she scrubbed at the dirt, trying to remove the stain. To her dismay, the damn thing refused to go away. Finally she gave up on the smudges. Perhaps the sisters would excuse her appearance once they knew what she and Hawk had endured.

Oh no! Her cheeks reddened and sweat seeped over her skin. What would they think when they found out she had once been a nun who broke her oath and left the abbey? Furthermore, it was not proper for a lass to be alone with a man as she had been. Would they think her a whore?

Kate abruptly stopped before she entered the keep when she recalled the white light coming from her hands as she'd fought off those two men, nay monsters, from the tavern. Certainly Hawk would keep that bit of information to himself until they had a chance to talk about it. Then again, he hadn't said a word about it. Mayhap he too would think her a witch.

Standing outside the keep, she looked up at the tall tower, amazed at its beauty and strength. There was a sense of serenity that surrounded the stone structure like a sanctuary. Even though charred chaos plagued the village, the keep was unscathed. Green ivy crept up the walls in a spray of lengthy vines like outstretched fingers. The stone shimmered in hues of gray and black. There was something most certainly magical about this place.

Once she was inside, the wonderment continued. Kate couldn't believe her eyes. This was everything she had envisioned a home would feel like—warm and inviting. Unlike the ruin outside, inside everything had a place and was kept exceptionally clean. Vibrant tapestries hung on the stone walls, telling tales of ancient battles. The smell of fresh pine brought her attention to the hearth where dark greenery covered the mantel. A wooden table stood in the middle of the room, groaning with provisions. Sconces were evenly placed along the walls and lit, casting a warm glow throughout the great hall.

Lana took Kate by the arm, leading her upstairs. Along the way Kate couldn't take her eyes away from more tapestries lining the walls.

"I have a bedchamber ready wit' a hot bath for ye." Lana leaned into Kate as she talked. "Gwen will be up wit' a few dresses as well."

Kate was surprised by Lana's kindness. "Thank ye. I am in need of a good bath." Kate brushed at a spot of dirt on her arm.

"Do no' fash yerself. I'm sure the journey was hard, knowing me brother. He's relentless when it comes to traveling through the Highlands."

Kate smiled. "Och, Hawk has been nothing but a gentleman, I can assure ye."

Lana chuckled. "Aye, a gentleman, but as grumpy as an auld goat."

Both woman burst out in laughter.

It was reassuring to Kate to have Lana be so kind. She pictured them getting along very well.

Lana stopped outside of a bedchamber door. "Here's yer room. Please take yer time. Evening meal will be ready shortly."

"Thank ye for being so kind, Lana. I—"

Lana excused her with a wave of a hand. "No need to thank me. A friend of Hawk's is a friend of mine." She smiled in a motherly way that warmed Kate's heart.

Lana spun on her heel and made her way back down the corridor as Kate opened the door to the bedchamber with the heavenly thought of a warm bath on her mind.

wen was right, the gold and green dress she had brought fit her perfectly. However it was still a foreign feeling not to be wearing her black tunic dress and veil. She

smoothed her hands down the front of the dress, fidgeting nervously.

The bath had been greatly appreciated by her sore, aching muscles and the lavender soap had relaxed her to the point that she had almost fallen asleep in the tub. Aye, Helmfirth seemed more and more like home.

As she took in more scenery from the great hall, she envisioned herself sitting around the table, gathered with Hawk's sisters and family, laughing and chatting. She even dared to dream about a family with him. She wondered what his favorite foods were, what made him happy, who crossed his mind when he was alone. She wanted to know his parents, who his friends were. But most of all she yearned to find a way to break down the wall around his heart.

As her thoughts ran away, realization crept in. Who was she fooling? She had thrown herself into Hawk's world and deep down, she knew she wasn't invited.

As she lost herself in the beauty of the keep, Lana slipped her arm around Kate. "Why dinnae ye help me in the kitchen? Looks like I have lost me help." Lana glanced at Gwen who was pretending to set the table as she stared toward the tall, dark stranger.

When they entered the kitchen the aroma of fresh baked bread was enough to make Kate's stomach growl and mouth water as Lana placed the loaves in a basket.

"So tell me, Kate, how did ye meet me brother?" Lana asked as she took a small cauldron off the flames.

Kate swallowed hard before she spoke. "Dunfermline Abbey. He appeared outside the gatehouse severely wounded and I helped him to the infirmary."

"Thank God, ye were there." Lana exhaled. "Are ye a nun then?"

This was the question she was dreading. "Aye, I was." Struck by the truth, Kate hung her head in shame.

"Och, lass, I do no' judge ye. Yer life is yers to live. I'm sure ye had a good reason to break yer vows." Lana handed Kate a basket of vegetables to chop. "And dinnae fash yerself. Yer secret is safe wit' me."

Kate took out a neep and began to prepare it. "Do ye know how Hawk was wounded? I've tried to ask him, but he's a man of few words."

Lana laughed. "Aye, he is." She paused as she thought of her next words carefully. "There was an attack on Helmfirth by this beast—"

"Lana, I'm sure Kate has better things to do than to listen to a tall tale." Hawk entered the kitchen, taking over their conversation. He grabbed a carrot from the basket and glared at Kate. "If it weren't for Kate and the monks at the abbey, I would have died." Lana and Kate fell silent. "In return, I'm taking Kate to Black Stone on the Hill."

"Och, I asked him to take me. He repaid his debt to the abbey by rebuilding the watermill. He did a fine job." Kate looked at Lana then back to Hawk, to catch another grave glare. "What aboot this beast?"

Hawk's brows furrowed. "It does no' matter to ye, Kate. Ye'll be leaving here soon, and ye'll be safe at Black Stone."

"She's safe here and can stay as long as she wants," Lana said as she stirred the soup in the cauldron.

"Lana, this be no business of yers. I vowed to take Kate to Black Stone and I will see it done."

Kate couldn't understand the change in Hawk. It seemed of late he he'd been showing a softer side, but as soon as he became aware of it, the soft edges became rough again. Deep down she wanted to stay. She wanted him to say that he wanted her to stay. "Really Hawk, there is no rush."

"As I said," Hawk pinned Kate with a forbidding stare, "I will see to it that ye arrive at Black Stone. We'll leave on the morrow."

Kate's blood boiled and her tongue twitched. He had pushed her too far this time. She tired of his stubborn nature and commands. They had just arrived. She wanted at least a day to explore and become more acquainted with his sisters—and to rest. She had left the nunnery to become her own woman, to make her own decisions. Nowhere did she remember agreeing to take orders from him.

Out of respect, though he didn't deserve it, Kate tamped down her anger and wiped her hands on her apron. "Well, as I see that my days have been planned out for me, I will excuse meself and wash up before the evening meal. I'll be heading to me bedchamber now."

"Of course, Kate," Lana said dolefully.

Before Kate left the kitchen, she glared long and hard at Hawk as she threw her apron on the table.

"Ramsey Comyn." Lana placed her hands on her hips and tapped her foot. "Da didnae raise ye to be an eejit."

"I be no eejit!"

His sister humphed. "I see the way Kate looks at ye. She likes ye and ye're turning her away just like everyone else in yer life."

"I know what ye're doing and I dinnae need ye interfering when it comes to a lass." Hawk exhaled, frustrated with his sister's meddling. "Ye can no' tell her aboot that wyvern that attacked the village. It will only open doors that I want to stay shut. Do ye understand me?"

"Nay, I do no' understand!" Lana was disgusted with her brother's stubbornness.

"What do ye suppose will happen when I tell a nun that I'm a dragon, a beastly devil in disguise, huh?"

Lana looked down at the floor remorsefully. "I dinnae know. Ye've never tried."

They both fell silent and a moment later Lana left the kitchen, leaving Hawk to stew in his own misery.

~

*H*awk sat at the head of the table with MacGregor by his side, brooding as usual. He was rather relieved to see his brother-in-law and second-in-command had survived the attack. MacGregor was a good man, for a human. As long as MacGregor made his sister happy that was all that mattered. As Hawk looked around he noticed the repercussions of the attack. Once the great hall would have been filled with laughter and people; now only a few remained, grimly eating and mourning their losses. Battle wounds were still fresh inside and out.

Hawk stirred and picked at his soup as he felt his people's despair.

He would rebuild Helmfirth and vowed never again to let his people down. This was his sisters' home and he would spend his days protecting the village.

Suddenly his body prickled and he was more aware of his surroundings. He looked up at the staircase as if he knew at that exact moment Kate would be coming down the stairs. The air in his lungs seized as he saw Kate descend. He was not going to watch her walk down with her short mahogany hair bouncing with each step she took, bringing attention to her long, slender neck. He was not going to think about running his tongue down her neck and nipping at her skin. He was not going to think about the green and gold dress she wore that hugged her body like a second skin. He was not going to think about kissing her exposed shoulders. *Shite!* He growled low and deep as Kate sat beside the tall, dark stranger and across from Gwen.

"Somethin' ails ye, brother?" Lana asked with a smirk as she took her seat next to her husband.

"I be well." *As long as I can resist the urge to cover Kate up with furs so no other man will be tempted to gaze upon her body.* Hawk took a hardy pull of his tankard of mead and shifted in his seat to relieve his aching cock. He was not going to give in to Kate. She deserved better. She deserved a man who was willing to give her his heart. Hawk was not that man; he was not capable of giving his heart away. After his mother's betrayal, he had built a stone wall around it for protection and there was no breaching that wall, as it was strong in resolve and cold as ice.

As the meal went on, he could feel Kate's eyes on him, yet he avoided her gaze. For he knew all it would take was one of her innocent smiles or the way she looked at him as if they were the only two people in the room to break him. Aye, he was treading a fine line.

Besides, he didn't need a lass invading his every thought. There were issues that needed to be addressed. First, who was this stranger who now sat next to Kate, making her laugh?

The evening meal had ended and Lana, Gwen, and Kate cleared the table and busied themselves in the kitchen, cleaning. Now was a good time to call forth a meeting. With their bellies full and the ale flowing, Hawk wasted no time and got right to the questions. "I think it be time that someone told me what happened here while I was gone." He leaned forward and clasped his hands together.

MacGregor cleared his throat. "How much do ye remember aboot the attack?"

"In the past few days bits and pieces have surfaced. I know that bloody wyvern must die," Hawk gritted through clenched teeth.

"After I placed ye on me horse, the wyvern destroyed more than half the village by its hellfire. That's when a dragon flew over Helmfirth, chasing the wyvern into the forest. I dinnae know if we would have survived if Rory had not come to our rescue. Which leads me to a question. Aye ye one too?" MacGregor nodded to Rory.

"Aye," Hawk confirmed.

Ever since that damn wyvern stepped claw in Helmfirth, there had been nothing but trouble. Hawk didn't trust this stranger any more than he trusted the wyvern. He stared intently at the man. "Ye be dragon?"

"Aye, I be Rory Cameron, one of the seven Guardians of Scotland and one hell of a Dragonkine warrior," he said with pride.

"Who sent ye here? How did ye know Helmfirth was under attack?" Hawk inquired.

"Our commander and chief, Sir James Douglas, sent me to inform ye of a deadly threat. I was no' expecting to see yer land under attack, but when I did—I got here just in time."

Hawk clenched his jaw, recalling the two-headed beast. "He and another man followed me and Kate to the tavern. They wanted Kate. Who are these men and why is Helmfirth under attack?"

"Marcus." Rory whispered. "This is no' good." He stood and paced the floor. "Tavish is the two-headed wyvern. I'm most certain he was sent here by Marcus to destroy you and Helmfirth in order to make their way into Govan.

"Hawk, ye need to heed my words and heed them well. Tavish has joined Marcus and they are building an army against our Kine to make certain the awakening of our true king, King Drest. And if he succeeds," Rory swallowed hard, "he will bring his vengeance down upon every human on his way to the Crown. He will destroy Scotland."

"Shite." MacGregor sighed.

"Who is this Marcus?" Hawk's brows furrowed.

Rory leaned forward. "Marcus was once a friend. He has turned against the Kine to awaken King Drest. For the longest time we didnae know he was a dragon, but now we know where his fidelity stands."

"And why would the Kine protect these humans? Why not stand by the Dragonkine King? He is dragon." Hawk glared at Rory sternly.

Rory blew out a breath. "Our commander, James Douglas, believes that humans should no' have to pay for something that happened centuries ago. And he's married to a human."

"I see."

"Trust me, Hawk, ye dinnae want to feel Drest's wrath. We need to come together and stop this tragic event."

There was a long pause as Rory and MacGregor waited for Hawk's response. "I dinnae understand why this involves me."

"Ye be Dragonkine; ye be one of the seven guardians. We need yer help to destroy Marcus so Drest willnae rise."

Hawk shook his head. "Nay, this be no' me war. I may be Dragonkine, but I'm no' guardian. I will no' risk my men, nor my people's lives. I have lost too many already."

"Hawk, ye have no choice. Drest will care naught who ye are. He will kill humans and dragons if ye dinnae join his fight. Together we can stop Marcus. And Drest."

Hawk slammed his fists on the table. Taking in a deep breath, he regained his composure. "I thank ye for coming to Helmfirth's aid, but I stand firm on my decision, I will no' join yer war." Hawk excused himself. As he was about to walk away, he turned back. "And ye best keep yer eyes off me sister, she's of no concern to ye."

Rory and MacGregor looked at one another as if they had given it their best effort to talk some sense into the laird. Rory didn't blame Hawk for his reaction, for he himself wasn't sure which side to take.

But he was tasked with warning Hawk, so he pushed his opinions aside and did what was commanded of him.

~

*H*awk wandered aimlessly around the keep, not sure what he was searching for, but he knew he hadn't found it yet. His happiness in returning home had been short-lived because of all this newfound information. There was much more to the attack than he realized. Indeed he was thankful for Rory coming to Helmfirth's aid, although he wasn't too keen on the man's affairs. Hawk would not risk going to war.

Then there was Kate. He wondered if she knew exactly who she was. If he had to guess, he would think not by the way she had reacted to her magic. But how could she not know? He paused for a moment as he heard a cry. Whoever it was they were in great pain. He heard the cry again and this time it sounded like a woman and it came from a bedchamber down the corridor. Kate?

16

*A*fter Kate helped with kitchen cleanup she couldn't wait to get back to her bedchamber and be alone, for she didn't know how long she could hold her tongue. During the evening meal she had fought the itch to give Hawk a piece of her mind. But he was the laird and surly with such a public display of a tongue-lashing there would have been severe consequences. She felt like an outsider because of the way he'd treated her. Throughout the evening meal he never glanced her way, not even once. In fact, she was indeed that outsider, looking in on his life, and this was not her home.

Kate sat down on the bed heavily. She'd left the abbey to find herself, not to fall in lust with the first man she laid eyes on. She looked at her hands; mayhap it was her. Hawk had seen a side of her she could not explain. There was magic flowing through her veins, but why? How? This had to be God's way of punishing her for leaving the abbey. A curse or a demon, damning her for life. She guessed she deserved it; she had gone against her vow, broken an oath to God. But it was too late to go back. All she could do was ask for forgiveness.

Kate knew what she had to do. It was what she had always done when she stepped off the path. When control had been lost. When boundaries had been broken. When temptation won over logic.

Walking over to her nightstand, she reached inside her satchel and pulled out the black leather whip. She stroked the leather strips hanging at the end of the handle, remembering and hating the biting sting of their strikes.

Kate laid the whip down on the bed and slipped her arms out of her dress, watching it fall to the ground. She stepped out from the green and gold material, grabbing the whip as she made her way in front of her dressing mirror. A controlled, impassive stare reflected back at her as she began her prayer to God. She raised her right hand and brought the whip's fury down onto her back. She winced in pain as blood trickled down. She repeated the motion again and again until she had matching slash marks. She cried out, and was waiting for the numbness to take over when someone knocked on her door.

"Kate, 'tis me, Hawk. Let me in." His voice urgent.

"Go away!" Kate yelled back.

"If ye dinnae open this door, I'll break it down. Now let me in!"

Kate frantically searched for a robe as she tried to stall him. "I told ye to go away! I do no' want yer company!"

Before she could finish her sentence, the door swung open with a crash and in stormed Hawk. "I heard ye cry out...God's bones!" Red angry slash marks marred her skin, reflecting through the mirror behind her. "Kate, what happened to ye?" Hawk grabbed her shoulders to turn her around but she slapped his hands away and darted from his reach. "Do no' touch me!"

Hawk snatched the whip from her hand. "Ye beat yerself...wit' this?" He shook the whip at her.

No more modest than a wee bairn running down the corridor naked, she quickly crossed her arms over her breasts. "Get oot! I didnae invite ye in. I'll—"

"Do what?" Hawk stalked her like wild game.

Pinned by his heated gaze, Kate backed into the wall. "I'll scream."

A breath away from her, he bent his head until his lips brushed against her cheek. "If ye scream, I'll scream too."

Kate looked up at the brawny Highlander and was opening her

mouth to scream when she saw he was making the same motion. She closed her mouth and again he followed. "Ye're an arse, Hawk," she whispered. "Nay, ye're a big, fat horse's arse."

He grinned. "Aye, I dinnae deny it." He brushed his thumb over her pouting lips. "Now, let me take care of ye and ye're going to explain this to me." Hawk held up the whip. "Go lie on the bed so I can tend to yer wounds."

Kate hesitated as he threw her whip into the blazing hearth. He took off his tunic and ripped it into strips. After he was done he fetched the wash basin. He halted when he saw that Kate was still standing in the corner. Sending her a stern glare, as if she was a disobedient child, he nodded to the bed.

Kate didn't know what it was about him that made her sweat every time he was around. Mayhap it was the roughness in his tone of voice. Mayhap it was the way his demanding presence filled a room. Mayhap it was his pure raw maleness. Whatever it was, she was attracted to it like bees to honey.

Kate gradually walked to the bed and lay down on her stomach, wincing as the pain struck her. Sitting beside her, Hawk proceeded to clean the cuts with his torn, wet tunic. Kate hissed and arched her back when the coldness of the rag wiped across the first wound.

"I be sorry," Hawk said as he continued cleaning the blood from her back. He bent down and blew lightly over her wounds. Goose-flesh prickled her skin and she shivered.

Kate looked over her shoulder. "Is Hawk yer given name?"

"Nay, Ramsey Comyn, son of the Red Comyn. Me sisters gave me the name Red Hawk. They teased me because of me red hair and me love for birds of prey."

Ramsey Comyn, she thought. *The name suits him well.* "Ramsey is a strong name."

"Och, lass, no' everyone knows me real name."

"Yer secret is safe wit' me." She smiled and began to fidget with the pillow. "Can I ask ye a question?" A grumble came from Hawk. "Have ye ever been in love?"

He finished cleaning her wounds then paused. He gathered up

the torn strips of tunic and the wash basin then left the bed. Kate rolled over on her side and was pleasantly surprised that she was no longer in pain. As she watched him dispose of the bloody rags by throwing them into the hearth, she thought perhaps she had scared him away by that question, until he strode back and lay down beside her.

Hawk looked up at the ceiling with his hands behind his head. "Nay, I have no'."

She faced him, resting her head on her hand. "Nor I. But I would like to know how it would feel to be thoroughly loved."

"And how do ye think that feels?"

Kate fell silent before she answered him. "'Tis two sparks creating a fire together."

They locked eyes. "'Tis a feeling of butterflies fluttering in yer stomach. 'Tis the way yer skin flushes when ye think aboot him."

Hawk rolled over on his side, facing her, wiggling his brows. "I think ye just described lust."

Kate playfully slapped his chest. "Do no' jest."

Hawk leaned in and placed his hand at the back of her neck, pressing his lips to hers ever so softly.

Kate closed her eyes and her body instantly come alive. Her skin burned for his touch, and something deep inside her begged him not to stop.

She grew impatient while he took his time kissing her cheek and down to her jaw. She leaned her head back and marveled in the sweltering trail of kisses he left down her neck. She thought she would explode.

"Och lass, do ye think love feels like this?" Hawk asked as he kissed her shoulder.

"Aye," she said breathlessly. "Aye." Claiming her lips once more, he deepened his kiss. She remembered their last kiss and how it had completely consumed her, but now it was different. The only thing between them was his plaid.

She felt his strong hands roam down the side of her ribs and up again. Her breath quickened as she felt him cup her breasts. She wanted more, she wanted all of him. Hawk broke their kiss and rested his forehead against hers as he thumbed over her nipple. "Ye're a verra bonny lass, Kate."

She threaded her fingers through his hair and kissed his forehead. "Hawk, ye make me feel bonny."

Suddenly he broke their embrace and rolled over on his back. Confused, Kate sat up. This was not the time for him to pull one of his brooding moments. If he left her in this state, she would go daft.

"Hawk, —"

"I've never been wit' a lass before," he said as he stared up at the ceiling.

He had never been with a lass, she thought. This explained a lot. Since Kate was still a virgin, she was relieved that Hawk was one as well.

"Nor I."

Hawk raised a brow.

She rolled her eyes and grinned. "I mean I have no' been wit' a man. But I do know one thing."

"What's that?"

She bent down and kissed his lips. "I want me first and only time to be wit' ye."

Before she knew what was happening, she was on her back, feeling his weight on top of her, turning that spark into a flame.

❧

*I*nexperience did not hold Hawk back. His skin prickled against Kate's touch as her hands traced the muscles down his chest. His blood pulsed aggressively with every kiss, every lick he placed on Kate's lips. His hands traveled her body, squeezing and teasing his fill. For the first time he truly felt alive.

He broke the whirlwind of lust that had taken his body and thoughts hostage. He took a moment to gather his breath as he stared down into the most beautiful hazel eyes he had ever seen. "Kate, are ye sure ye want this? Because if we go any further I won't be able to stop."

A part of him wanted her to throw him out of the bedchamber. He wanted her to hate him, curse his name. There was no place in his heart for a lass, yet with Kate it was different. He took her head in his hands and caressed her rosy cheeks. Aye, he wanted Kate and his dragon wanted to stake his claim.

Wait...his dragon? Aye, it was him stirring from within. Every touch from Kate brought out more and more of the dragon. She was bringing him back to life.

The hunger was in her eyes as she looked up at him through thick lashes. He prayed to the Gods that Kate wanted him as much as he wanted her.

"Aye, I do," she whispered in his ear.

Dizzy with desire, he fumbled unfolding his plaid, then paused as he felt Kate's shaking hands on top of his, encouraging him to undress. She was nervous, he thought. Hell, they were both a bundle of frayed nerves ready to come undone.

Kate's eyes roamed down his chest, his abdomen, and to his length then back up to him.

Maintaining eye contact, Hawk reassured her. "We'll take it slow. I promise, lass, I willnae hurt ye."

"I trust ye." Kate licked her lips and that was the last thread of control to unravel.

Feverishly, he claimed her lips as her nails left erotic trails of passion down his shoulders and back. Her touch drove him daft with desire. Leisurely he trailed his hand down her long slender leg and back up to her inner thigh. God's bones, her body was luscious and soft. His dragon purred from deep inside and awakened something primal inside him. *Claim the lass.*

Craving more, he delicately trailed his finger down her silken folds; he had never felt anything so soft and delicate in his life. Watching Kate's blushing cheeks and the way she licked her lips and moaned as he slid his finger deep inside her, he knew she wouldn't last long.

"Hawk," Kate panted. "Do ye feel the tingles running through yer body?"

"Aye, I do believe me body has been bewitched."

He continued his sweet torture on her body until he felt like he was going to burst from the inside out. Kissing and touching her became an addiction. He couldn't stop, nor did he want to. But if he didn't find a way to rein in his desire for a while and live in the moment, he would be done before he started. Taking in a deep breath, he had everything under control until he felt soft, gentle strokes on his sleek length and the soft-spoken words in his ear. "Hawk, I need ye." Kate moaned and kissed his neck.

Surprised by her dauntless actions, he grabbed her hands and placed them over her head, keeping his hand on hers. "If ye keep touching me like that, lass, it will be over."

Kate looked up at him, her breath hitched in her chest. "And if ye dinnae make love to me now I can no' be held responsible for me actions."

"Och, lass." He chuckled. "Yer wish is my command."

Positioning himself betwixt her legs, he guided himself in and broke down all boundaries between them. Kate's body tensed and the sting of her nails bit into his back as he pushed forward. Undoubtedly, this was going to hurt her and he felt like an arse because he was to blame for it, yet there was a sense of honor deep within him that she wanted to give her virginity to him.

She wrapped her legs around his waist, encouraging him to proceed. Before he buried himself to the hilt he whispered in her ear, "Ye honor me, lass."

Surrender had never felt so good.

~

A wave of tingles crashed into Kate as Hawk pressed into her womanhood. She felt the bitter sting inch by inch, yet she wanted more. Nothing was going to stand in the way of this moment. As soon as their bodies became one she was more than ever positive she had made the right choice, to give herself to this man. Every kiss, touch, and thrust felt right.

Kate wrapped her arms around his neck as Hawk found a rhythm that pushed them both closer to pleasures they had never experienced before. She made delightful moans and murmurs, for she didn't know what to say to him. All she knew was she didn't want him to stop.

Tingles kept building up and in one last thrust her body let go of everything she was holding on to. Stars burst behind her closed eyes. Waves rippled through her all the way down to her toes. Warmth like sun rays beaming down on her filled her body and all hope of gaining control of her being faded as she gave herself to Hawk.

The last wave surfaced and his body tensed beneath her and filled her from deep inside. "By the saints, Kate," he gasped as he nuzzled her neck.

Time halted as they stayed as one. Kate didn't know what to do, but stay in this moment right here with Hawk. She didn't want this night to end, though the real world waited to take this time away from her. Having no claim on him, she hoped that maybe after tonight things would be different between them. Perhaps he would want her to stay at Helmfirth. Was that too much for a lass to dream about?

Hawk stirred and lay down beside her. As soon as he left her, she felt alone again and missed his warmth. She watched him leave the bed and walk over to the wash basin. Was he leaving? Please God, she hoped he would at least stay through the night. Without saying a word, which was driving Kate daft, he returned with a wet cloth. Kate lay back and allowed Hawk to pull the covers back and expose her naked body. Cold wetness bit at her skin, causing her flesh to prickle as he began to wipe her virginal blood from her inner thighs. Being as still as a frightened doe in the woods, she watched him gently wash her. "Did I hurt ye, Kate?" He looked up at her with remorseful eyes and it broke her heart.

Kate sat up, pulling the cover over her body. She took his hand in hers. "Nay, I have never felt something so…so wonderful before. What did ye do to me?" She smiled.

He took her hands and brought them up to his lips. "Ye are a verra bonny lass. I dinnae know what I would do if I caused more pain than ye've already had to endure."

"I'm no' that delicate. I won't break if ye touch me." Kate smiled and pulled him down on the bed next to her. "I do hope ye'll be staying the night wit' me."

Situating himself under the furs, he wrapped his hulking arms around Kate and drew her in closer to his body until she fit perfectly next to him. "Och, lass, I will no' leave ye. Besides I know how ye hate sleeping alone. I would only find ye in me bed later." He grinned and kissed the top of her head.

She playfully jabbed him with her finger. "I can no' help it. Ye make me feel safe."

"Good, now get some sleep." Hawk yawned.

Kate nuzzled next to him, placing her head on his chest. She was giddy with joy, so much so that she couldn't sleep. All she could think about was a future with Hawk. She knew she could make a new life here. She envisioned herself helping Hawk's sister to make Helmfirth once again the home it used to be. And if she looked further, perhaps a wee bairn or two. All the years spent at the abbey feeling as if something nay, someone was missing in her life, and now she had found him. It was Hawk.

"Hawk." Kate looked up at him and traced his jawline with her finger.

"Kate, get some rest."

Sensing he was in no mood for sentimental chatter, Kate kissed his chest. "I love ye, Ramsey Comyn."

17

*S*weat soaked his sheets as Kate's voice kept repeating in his head, *I love ye, Ramsey Comyn.* The night had been long and sleep had been elusive as his problem lay snugly next to him. Throughout the hours of darkness, Hawk thought about how he was going to let the lass go, yet he found himself hitting a stone wall. Being a man who never surrendered to anyone, his life of solitude was a choice he had maintained for most of his life and he had no room in it for a lass.

Dragons weren't welcomed in everyday society. Yet he had done the unexpected and had grown quite fond of Kate, which wasn't sitting well with him at the moment. No one, not even his sisters, could make him smile the way Kate could. She had crawled under his skin and made him feel alive, which was an odd feeling. But every time he thought that maybe, just maybe, a life with her was within his reach, a small problem surfaced and prevented him from thinking further into the future; he was dragon who wasn't capable of giving his heart away.

In addition, there was still a threat out there: the two men from the tavern. They wanted Kate, but for what he did not know. Mayhap it had something to do with her special ability to blast people on their arses. So the best option for her would be to stay here at Helm-firth so he could protect her. He could keep her close, yet far enough away that he could love her from a distance. Nay, he thought, she would find her way to him, especially at night. She hated sleeping alone.

He cursed himself for a coward. If he could, he would confess his true identity. She had awakened something within him and the thought of taking her to Black Stone lay heavy on his heart. Sweat began to bead across his forehead again as he sat up in bed, careful not to awaken her. Mayhap he should tell her today and be done with it. Then she would want to leave.

A crack of morning sun shined in the bedchamber as Hawk slipped out of bed and wrapped his plaid around his waist. A rumble from his stomach echoed through the chamber, which gave him an idea. There was no need to confess right away. They could start the day off with breaking their fast in bed. Hawk shook his head, knowing he was procrastinating as he looked over at Kate sleeping like an angel.

He took the stairs two at a time. As he reached the great hall he heard chattering—voices he didn't recognize. His pace quickened when he heard Kate's name mentioned. Had those two bastards from the tavern caught up with them? Nay, not even a dragon could breach the doors of the keep.

"Och, good morning, sunshine," Rory greeted him.

Hawk shot Rory a look that would pin him dead. "Dinnae call me sunshine again and who in the devil are they?" He pointed at the couple who sat across from Rory.

"Is Kate going to join us this morn?" Rory folded his arms over his chest, avoiding eye contact.

"This is my home and I'll be asking the questions. Besides, what does Kate have to do with this? I want to know why these strangers were allowed in my home without me knowing aboot it." Hawk's tone became more and more belligerent the further Rory pushed him.

"Hawk, I mean ye no disrespect, but ye may want to sit down. Hell, grab a dram, for what we're aboot to tell ye changes everything."

~

*K*ate rolled over, expecting Hawk to be lying next to her. The sheets were cold. She sat up with urgency, thinking the worst. Her veins pulsed with heat. She clutched her amulet. She remembered having the same burning sensation back at the tavern before she felt the magic overtake her. Was she going to do it again? Right here, right now?

Kate jumped out of bed and ran to the wash basin, splashing fresh water on her face. The cool water soothed her and she started to calm down. The skin on her arms and chest tingled and itched. What was happening to her? Looking in the mirror, she rubbed her hands up and down her arms, looking for the scroll markings, yet she found none. She breathed a sigh of relief. "'Tis nothing." Then she remembered Hawk tending to the wounds that were left behind from the whip. Turning so her back faced the mirror, Kate covered her mouth to hold back a scream. There were no wounds visible. Not even a scratch. "By the saints," she said, astonished.

Quickly, she searched for a gown and shoes. She needed to find Hawk and finally figure out what in the devil was going on.

There was no time to waste as Kate rushed down the corridor, stumbling about while she slipped on her last shoe. She reached the stairs but stopped abruptly. Voices came from the great hall and one of them was Hawk's.

"Hawk, Kate is special." She didn't recognize that voice. Who was here and how did they know her? No one from the abbey would have traveled this far just for her. She took the stairs slowly one by one, keeping quiet and listening to every last word.

Hawk refused to sit. He stood with his arms crossed over his chest in a defensive stance. "What do ye mean, 'special'?"

The long red-haired man sitting next to a beautiful woman poured himself a dram before he said, "It appears our friend here," he nodded his head to Rory, "has failed to introduce us. I'm Magnus, one of the seven Guardians and this be Fia. She's our kind. She's a Dragonkine female."

Hawk glared at Fia. She had a familiar beauty about her eyes "So ye be dragon, aye? If ye're here to talk me into yer war, ye're terribly mistaken. I've already told yer friend that I be no interested."

"Och, laddie, I believe ye will change yer mind. Ye see, Kate is me daughter—"

"And I'm her mother," Fia interrupted. "Why did ye take her from the abbey?"

"Och, she left of her own free will. In fact she asked me to take her to Black Stone to see a friend. Do no' blame me for her actions." Hawk worked his jaw as he was taken aback by this newfound information. "How do I know ye speak the truth?"

Fia stood and took off her cloak. Shimmering pink Celtic scrolls covered her arms. Hawk stared, astonished. They were the same markings Kate had back at the tavern, yet hers were white. He followed the scrolls up to her face, where familiar hazel eyes looked back at him. Could it be? "I'm Kate's mother and I assure ye that Magnus is her father. The two men at the tavern were there to kill ye and take Kate. They want something she has."

Kate couldn't believe what she was hearing as she reached the last stair. She turned to walk away, but bumped into an unlit torch mounted on the wall next to her. The torch fell to the ground with an echoing thud. "Shite." Surprised by her exclamation, she covered her mouth.

"Kate? Is that ye?" Hawk called out and strode toward her.

She closed her eyes and took in a breath. It was too late to run and hide. They all knew she was here. "Aye."

Hawk took her hand in his. "Ye need to come wit' me."

"Nay, I have heard enough." Even though she was curious about her parents, her instincts were protecting her, telling her to run. This man was dragon?

"Kate, listen to me." He bent down until their eyes met. "Ye need to listen to what they have to say. I'll be right here wit' ye."

Reluctantly, Kate followed Hawk into the great hall. The woman in white slowly stood from the table. As Kate studied the woman she recognized the markings. The scrolls were wrapped around her arms and while Kate's were white, the woman's were tinged pink. "Kate, me name is Fia and I'm yer—"

"I know. I've heard everything." Kate crossed her arms over her chest. "And ye be me da?" She nodded to Magnus.

"Aye, lass, and may I say I'm honored to finally meet ye." Magnus smiled as any proud father would.

Minutes seemed to turn into hours and they all succumbed to uncomfortable silence. Kate sat at the table, not knowing what to say, staring down into her lap where her hands were folded and fidgety. There were too many questions floating around in her head, making it spin. Dragons did not exist and magic was a fool's belief, she thought. Even though she had felt the magic, it couldn't be true.

Kate looked at her mother then to her father with tears threatening to spill. "Why?" Her voice shook. "Why did ye leave me?"

Fia sorrowfully glanced at Magnus then back to Kate. "I know ye will never forgive me and mayhap ye'll never understand me actions, but I had to protect ye, my love." Fia paused and inhaled deeply. "There are beings oot there who wanted us dead because of who we are. They wanted our light, our power to awaken a tyrant. I became tired of running from village to village, so I decided to hide ye at Dunfermline Abbey."

"And what aboot this?" Kate showed her mother the amulet.

Fia dropped her gaze to the floor. "I placed a spell bound by blood so that yer true identity would be hidden as long as ye wore the necklace. Ye wouldn't experience any of yer powers."

Puzzled, Kate's brows furrowed "What do ye mean my true identity?"

"Ye are a Dragonkine female, Kate. Ye are one of us."

Kate's eyes widened. "I'm a dragon?"

Fia smiled and shook her head. "We are mates of the Dragonkine. We have powers that help protect them. Without us," Fia glanced at Magnus, "their dragons could very well become unruly and destructive. They need us to survive."

"Aye," Magnus spoke up. "Rory, myself, and Hawk here—we be dragons. Ye mother and ye hold special powers, but no dragon."

Thinking back to the tavern, Kate brought her hands in front of her, and examined them thoroughly. "Then this explains the blast of white light."

"What do ye mean?" Fia asked.

Hawk placed his hand on Kate's shoulder, giving the poor lass comfort. "There were two men who followed us to the tavern on our way to Helmfirth. They tried to attack me. That's when Kate blasted them with her magic."

"Shite." Rory ran his hand through his hair.

"Aye, they know who she is." Magnus slammed his fist on the table.

"Who?" Hawk asked.

"Marcus," both Rory and Magnus answered.

"He's the one I was telling ye aboot. He wants to awaken Drest." Rory stood and walked over to a window. "He's oot there now. I can feel his evil."

Trembling, Kate asked, "Why me?"

With sorrowful eyes Fia looked at her daughter. "He wants the blood that is around yer neck."

Magnus pulled on his beard in deep thought. "Aye, it makes sense. Since he has failed to kill a dragon on holy ground, he's looking for an easier way. If he captures Kate then he has what he needs to awaken the king."

Kate grabbed her amulet and tugged. "Och, he can have it. I dinnae want this."

"Nay! Stop! Dinnae remove the amulet." Fia stood and raced over to her daughter. She bent down in front of Kate and held her hands. "He will find ye if ye remove it."

Surprised, Kate removed her hands from the necklace.

"If ye remove it, any Dragonkine warrior can find ye."

"Can't ye undo the spell?" This was all too much for Kate to take in. Sweat beaded across her forehead. This all had to be a dream and she would wake up any minute, aye?

Magnus stood behind Fia and peered at his daughter. "Do no'

fash yerself, lass, we are here to protect ye. We dragons protect our own with our lives, that ye can be certain of."

"Aye, we want to take ye to Black Stone where ye'll be safe," Fia said.

Hawk cleared his throat.

Kate could see hope in her mother's eyes, but deep down she didn't want to leave. The attraction she felt toward Hawk now made sense. She was Dragonkine female; she had powers of her own. Hawk was a dragon; surely he would want her to stay at Helmfirth? He could keep her safe. She glanced at Hawk as if she was waiting for him to say something. She waited and prayed that he would intervene and tell them she would be safe here with him. But there was nothing said as she watched Hawk turn and walk away.

Kate stood. "Excuse me." She followed him into the solar where she found him in front of the hearth with his hands gripping the mantel. She walked in slowly. "Say something, Hawk."

"What is it that ye want me say?" His voice was grim.

"I dinnae know."

Hawk spun around and grabbed her by her waist. "I do know what ye want me to say. Ye want me to say I want ye to stay here, that I will protect ye. Dinnae ye?" He lightly shook her to get his point across. "Ye want me to say that I love ye. Kate...I can no'..."Hawk shook his head.

Tears ran down her face as she looked up into his dark swirling eyes.

"Ye now know what I am. 'Tis best that ye go." Hawk took a step back.

Of course she knew he was a dragon, nothing had changed her feelings for him. If what they had told her was true, then she was meant to be with a dragon. But why was he denying her? Why couldn't he just tell her his true feelings? Because she was dealing with a stubborn dragon that's why. Mayhap she was seeing more than what was really in front of her. Mayhap he really didn't want her here, nor in his life.

"Is it because ye dinnae want me?" Kate tried to look him in the eyes but Hawk stared at the ground.

"Nay, I can no' protect ye like yer father and mother."

Downhearted and angered, Kate unleashed her fury and pushed him. "Ye're a liar, Hawk!" When he didn't budge from the blow she pushed him again. "A big arse of a liar!" Kate wiped the tears from her cheeks. "After everything we have shared, ye're still too stubborn to tell me."

Hawk stood motionless. Kate squared her shoulders and lifted her chin, and gathered what dignity she had left. She wasn't going to make a bigger fool of herself than she already had. If he wanted her gone then so be it, she would leave. "If ye have nothing more to say to me, then I'll be on my way."

Kate strode out the door. She needed some fresh air and to stay clear of that arse of a man, yet there was still a part of her that wanted him to change his mind and tell her what she wanted to hear. Again there was only silence.

18

The air was thick, and Kate felt as if the castle walls were closing in on her. Crossing the great hall, she could feel everyone's eyes on her, especially her mother's. She needed to be alone and far away from these people. Her head spun, her heart raced and her lungs tightened, making it hard to breathe. It took all of her will to keep her composure until she got outside.

As soon as she opened the double wooden doors, she ran. She darted toward the forest, passing tree after tree, stumbling over small rocks. Hiking up her skirts, she pumped her legs faster in a full on run. Even low-lying branches that cut into her face and tangled her hair didn't stop her.

Running until her legs buckled, she fell to her knees. With her head in her hands, she sobbed and gasped for air, letting her sorrows break free. In a short amount of time her whole world as she knew it had spun out of control. Her whole life had been a lie. She was never meant to live the abbey life, and her soul knew it. Finding out that she was a Dragonkine female, meeting her mother and father for the first time, and then falling in love with a dragon was more than she could handle. Why did she have to love a dragon?

A flock of black birds flew above her, peppering the sky and causing a disturbance in the forest. Kate glanced up at the squawking birds and followed them with her eyes toward a loch, where they landed in a nearby tree. Odd, she thought, she hadn't noticed it before. Wiping the tears from her face, Kate stood slowly. Her legs burned and ached as she took a step in the direction of the loch. The thought of fresh, cold water drove her and she picked up the pace.

When she finally reached her destination she bent down and collected water in her cupped palm, drinking her fill. She splashed her face and the back of her neck. The loch was so inviting that she took her shoes off and submerged her feet in the water. The coolness soothed her throbbing feet and the sound of the waves crashing against the shore calmed her soul.

She had run heedlessly, wildly, yet no matter how far she went, her heart still ached and her world still spun. What was she going to do? She now knew that her mother hadn't abandoned her at the abbey; Fia had been protecting her. The beaming look her mother had given her back at Helmfirth was enough to make Kate smile. *She really does care.* And her da was handsome with his long red hair and beard to match. Something deep inside her confirmed that she belonged to them. As a matter of fact, all her life she had known she was different.

Kate kicked at the water as she walked along the loch's edge. Perhaps leaving with them to go to Black Stone was wise; perhaps it was where she needed to be. She would be protected and Abigale would be there. *Abigale.* She couldn't wait to see her. Maybe she could give her words of wisdom on how to heal a broken heart. Kate huffed. *Ramsey Comyn.* Why had she given her heart to such an unmanageable man? In his world she had no meaning, for if she did, surely he would have fought to keep her at Helmfirth.

Be strong, Kate. She tried to be her best supporter. Leaving the abbey was supposed to bring her freedom, a way to find her true self. Now it was time to move forward and leave Hawk behind. In time her heart would heal, yet the scars would always be there, reminding her of her short-lived time with him. She would never thoroughly forget him.

Kate didn't know how long or how far she had walked when she stopped and looked up from the shoreline. It was peaceful out here, serene. In a way she wished she could stay forever. As she peered over the loch, she wrapped her hands around her amulet, twirling it carefully in her hand. *Dragons?* She shook her head in disbelief, then realized she shouldn't be out here alone. There were two men after her, meaning her harm.

Like a little lamb staring into a wolf's gray hungry eyes, Kate's heart skipped a beat. She needed to get back to Helmfirth—her life depended on it. Before she could turn back, an image of something hunched over by the water's edge came into view. Although Kate couldn't get a clear view, the image looked frail and petite; it was a woman. She knew she should be on her way, but Kate couldn't bear the thought of leaving without at least asking the woman if she was well.

With a quickening stride, Kate cautiously approached the woman. "Pardon me."

Startled, the woman stood and pulled her cloak tightly around her.

"I'm sorry, I didnae mean to scare ye." As Kate studied the woman she could see that she must be no more than ten-and-eight. Her long hair shined a honey gold against the sun rays. There was something familiar about her, yet Kate knew she had never met the young lass. "Are ye well? Do ye need help?"

The lass shook her head as she looked into the forest tree line as if she was waiting for something to come out of the woods. Kate followed the woman's eyes. She hadn't heard anything, not even the crack of a branch when she approached.

The lass moved closer to Kate and whispered, "They're watching."

Kate's eyes widened and her heart sped up. "What do ye mean?"

"Shhhh. They can hear us." The lass looked again into the woods then back to Kate. "Ye should no' be here. They are looking for ye."

The hairs on the back of Kate's neck bristled. Every fiber of her being was telling her to run, yet her feet wouldn't move. The blood pulsed all the way up to her ears, pounding so hard she couldn't hear.

"Go. Walk away slowly and whatever ye do, dinnae make a sound," the lass warned.

Inhaling deeply, Kate slowly turned around and began walking the shoreline as if nothing had happened. With every step she took, she prayed that she would make it safely back to Helmfirth. She dared a glance over her shoulder to see if the lass was still there and she was. Then her eyes shot to the tree line as four men came charging at the lass. She watched as they grabbed her and pushed her to the ground. Dear God! Were they going to kill her?

Fighting the urge to go help, Kate did exactly what she had been told. As she turned back round she bumped straight into a man's chest. Looking up, she screamed in terror. It was Marcus, the man from the tavern.

"Shh." He pressed his gloved fingers over his lips, hushing her.

Terrified to the marrow, Kate didn't move.

"I see that ye've been warned about me." He shook his head, disgusted at the thought. "Truly, I'm growing weary of these tiresome rumors."

Quickly, Kate threw her hands in front of her, calling forth her powers, but alas there was nothing. Stunned, she looked at her hands. How could this be? Where was her magic when she needed it?

A bellowing laugh came from Marcus. "Ye silly lass. Do ye actually think I'll let ye blast me again with yer magic? And ye forgot one small detail. Ye're wearing the blood of a dragon around yer neck."

From behind her one of his men grabbed her hands and tied them behind her back. Kate struggled against his hold. How could she have been so stupid?

Smiling with an evil twist, Marcus slowly took off his black glove, exposing his bare hand. He cupped her face and her blood chilled. His hand turned blue and she felt the cold bite into her cheeks. "Ye'd best save yer powers. Ye'll need yer strength once Drest is done wit' ye."

The man from behind shoved her forward as they headed back into the forest. What was she going to do? There was no escaping. "She rides wit' her." Kate glanced at where Marcus was pointing and saw the lass with one of the men from the loch, walking toward a horse. The burly man snarled and picked the lass up and placed her on the horse, then he turned to Kate. He was cloaked in black and his face was shadowed by darkness. She could feel the malevolence that surrounded him. *Could this be the evil that chased me and me mother years ago?* He took long, heavy strides toward her and she swore she could hear the ground thunder. "We've finally caught ye, wench," he sneered. "It has been a long time coming, but we got ye." Desperate to get away from him, Kate took a step back, but was pushed forward by the man standing behind her.

"What are ye waiting for, get her on the horse. Now!" Marcus commanded as he sat perched on his massive warhorse, waiting to lead the way.

Before Kate knew what was happening, she was picked up and flung over the man's shoulder, then placed behind the lass on a black horse. Once the man left to mount his own horse, the woman whispered over her shoulder, "Do no' flash yerself, Kate, I know who ye are." The young woman slid her cloak off her shoulder, revealing white scroll marks.

Kate gasped. How could this be, and what in the devil was going on? The lass clicked her horse forward, following Marcus closely as they made their way through the thicketed forest.

With every stride the horse took, Helmfirth became smaller and smaller and Kate fell deeper into despair. No one would find her out here, hidden from the worn path. If she didn't escape now she would never make it back to Helmfirth. But how? She couldn't outrun these men or whatever they were; she wasn't physically strong enough. And screaming would earn her a gag. She had no weapons on her person, so what options were left? Her mind. She had to keep strong and outwit them. Even though of late she was beginning to doubt her past judgment, she had to stand her ground. There was no time to dwell in self-pity.

Then the thought arose as she clenched her amulet. *Mayhap my father, Rory, or Hawk could find me if I took off the amulet.* She was already in the hands of the enemy, furthermore her mother had

warned that a Dragonkine could find her if she removed her necklace. That's right, she thought. Remove the amulet and use her
powers. Either way she had to do something. She struggled with the
rope that bound her hands. If only she could break free.

"If I were ye I wouldn't let them see what ye're doing," the
lass said.

Kate paused. She didn't know if she could fully trust her.

"Who are ye?" Kate asked.

"Me name is Aela."

"Why are ye here? Did he hurt ye?"

"Ye ask too many questions, Kate."

"So I've been told," Kate huffed.

"I was captured on my way back home to the realm."

"Realm?"

"Aye, our home," Aela answered, puzzled that Kate didn't know
about it. "Ye dinnae know about our home?"

"Nay, my identity has been kept a secret from me all me life."

"'Tis best ye dinnae know aboot it. Ye'd never want to leave. I wish
I hadn't." Aela looked straight ahead, emotionless, yet Kate could feel
her sorrow. She had to get them out of this mess somehow.

She looked behind her. There were two of Marcus's men riding
side by side, glaring at her as if they were daring her to try to escape.
She thought it better not to give them what they wanted, her running
for her life while they chased and taunted her as if she was their play
toy. Nay, she needed her magic or Aela's. That's if she could trust her.

"Aela?" Kate said. "Do all Dragonkine females possess the
same magic?"

Aela stiffened in her saddle. "Shh. Ye must no' talk aboot it.
There's no escaping."

"Are ye telling me that ye want to stay here with these...these
monsters?" Kate leaned forward and whispered into Aela's ear, "We
must stick together. We have to at least try to escape."

Aela remained silent, which made Kate nervous. Had she dug her
own grave, admitting that she had powers? God, she hoped not.

They traveled in silence through the night, following the light of the moon deep within the Highlands. They trod up and down small inclines of dirt and rock. They tracked a stream that poured from the top of a mountain and still there was no sign of stopping.

Again Kate tried to loosen the ropes that bound her hands. She wiggled and twisted her hands until the rope bit into her wrist, but that wasn't going to stop her efforts. She had to break free.

The two men who rode behind her trotted past to the front of the line where Marcus was leading. The horses came to a halt. Marcus and his men seemed to be in an intense conversation by the way they pointed fingers and clenched their jaws. This was her opportunity; she had to break free.

"Please, Aela, we dinnae have much time, help me break the rope," Kate begged and pleaded and yet Aela stood firm, emotionless, staring straight in front of her.

Kate exhaled, trying not to accept defeat, but it appeared her fate was sealed until she felt the rope loosening around her wrist. Strands of it twisted and unknotted enough that she could slip her hands free. "Thank ye, Aela."

"Ye best no' leave me behind," Aela threatened.

Kate smiled. "Ye have me word."

She didn't know if she was making the right decision, but if she was going to be held captive, she was going to fight. Slowly Kate reached up and lightly held the amulet. She paused and sent a plea to God that she and Aela would make it out of the mess alive. As she tugged at the egg-shaped locket, the leather snapped and broke free from her neck. She leaned her head back and closed her eyes. *Please, Hawk, find me.*

19

*W*hy did his sister have to be right? He was an eejit. Nay, Kate had been right: an arse. Hawk aggressively ran his hand through his hair as he paced the solar. Why couldn't he tell her what she wanted to hear? He didn't want to let her go, that was certain. He felt it all the way down to his dragon. The way her eyes teared with hurt tore at his heart, or where his heart should be. How could he have been so senseless as to let her go?

Hawk strode over to the wooden desk that sat in the middle of the room and punched his fists into the top. He leaned into his arms as he rested them on the table, rocking back and forth calling himself the fool of fools. This was why he'd vowed to stay clear of lasses. He was incapable of loving another. He had proven it by the way he had overreacted to Kate.

His dragon stirred and groaned, wanting to shift. The beast wanted to rear its head, he wanted to find Kate and bring her home. Hawk growled as fury ripped through him. His claws extended, puncturing the wood as he gripped the desk and flipped the bloody thing over. He spun around and pinned his rage on a nearby chair. With haste he grabbed it and threw it across the room, sending it crashing against the door. Everything he placed his sights on shattered against a wall or was bashed into the ground. Nothing in the solar was safe from Hawk's wrath.

With nothing else to destroy, he leaned against the stone wall, his legs weakened, and slid down onto the floor. He was slouched over with his legs stretched out in front of him. He was a broken man. "She's gone."

He leaned his head back and glared at the ceiling. What was he going to do? Could he actually live without Kate in his life? He straightened his head and glanced across at the rubble of splintered wood and broken furniture. Nay, as much as he deny it, he couldn't. He needed her like fire needed flames. Like his dragon needed to fly.

Hawk pushed himself up. He had to go find Kate and right the wrong. He couldn't let her leave under these circumstances. His father had taught him to be a better man. Then if she still wished to leave, he would let her go. Whatever the outcome may be, it would be up to Kate.

Stepping over the wreckage, he made his way to the door and walked out. With haste, he took the stairs two at a time up to Kate's bedchamber. It was the first place that came to mind, knowing she was packing for Black Stone.

"Kate." He knocked on the door and knocked louder when there was no reply. "Kate, open the door. We need to talk." It was no surprise that she didn't want to, frankly he expected it, but she would listen to what he had to say. "Kate, if ye dinnae open this door, I'm breaking the bloody thing down." Hawk waited then he tried opening the door. To his disbelief it wasn't locked. He crossed the threshold and entered the bedchamber. The bed was neatly made and her dress was clean and draped across the foot of it. As he nervously made his way across the room his eyes narrowed in on her dressing table. Her hairbrush lay on the table as if it hadn't been used since the morn. "Kate!" As he turned his well-built body around to search the room his shin slammed into the corner of a metal object. "Shite!" He glared down at the blasted thing. It was her trunk that Gwen had filled with dresses and gowns. He opened the trunk. Everything was here. Hawk rubbed the tension from the back of his neck.

She hadn't packed, which meant she hadn't left yet. Hawk exhaled. "Where are ye, Kate?"

He called out to her one more time before quitting the bedchamber. With long purposeful strides, he strode down the corridor, determined to find her. She had to be here somewhere.

A shiver ran up his spine and Hawk froze. The shiver was replaced by a sting that shot straight to his core. He bent over, clutching at his stomach. As quickly as it started, the sensation stopped. What in the devil was happening to him? As he straightened, he felt her. Starting from his toes and working its way up his body directly to his head, hot prickles stung his skin.

However, these tingles were nothing like last night's. They felt as if hundreds of bees were stinging him from the inside and carried a terrible sense of danger. The sudden urgency to find Kate consumed him as he bolted down the stairs and burst through the great hall. Magnus shot up from where he was sitting when he saw Hawk running to the door. "Ye felt it too, aye?"

"Aye, 'tis Kate and she's in danger." Hawk opened the doors to the keep and surveyed the graying horizon.

Taking off his tunic, Rory stood beside him. "Do no' fash yerself. We'll find her, me brother."

"Aye." Magnus stood on Hawk's other side. "Rory's the best tracker we have. If anyone can find her, 'tis him."

Hawk looked at Rory then back to Magnus and hung his head. "I mean ye no disrespect, but I know Kate...physically. I know her scent."

Saying more than any words could, Magnus flashed his deep green hazel eyes at Hawk. "Ye...mated wit' me daughter?"

"I...dinnae think she is me mate. I just know her scent."

"Ye fool!" Magnus grabbed Hawk by his tunic and bared his teeth. "The only way ye know her scent and can feel her is because she is yer mate."

Not allowing his anger to show, Hawk took a step back. Aye, he was a fool by all means, however this fool was going to bring Kate back.

Meaningfully, Hawk ripped his tunic off his chest and tore his plaid from his body and took off in a fast sprint toward the forest. Within seconds his spine popped vertebra by vertebra. Arms turned into wings and his skin scaled red. His deep dark brown eyes swirled red with intensity and his irises morphed into slits. His human body succumbed to his beast.

With elongated strides the beast thundered through the glen bending branches and uprooting trees, gaining enough speed to take to the sky with only one thing on his mind—to rescue Kate.

20

*M*arcus rode ahead through the auld kingdom of Govan leisurely, yet on guard, surveying the barren land. "Spread out," he commanded the band of Creepers.

Overgrown vines and weeds covered a skeleton, where once had stood a magnificent stronghold. Chunks of stone littered the ground in crumbles, reminding Marcus of a battle that had ended a legacy of dragons. Centuries of aging could never hide the brutality the humans had left behind. The wind blew sour here and if one were to listen carefully, voices of old could be heard moaning a tune of misery. This was holy land.

Marcus dismounted. A chill shot over him as soon as his feet hit the ground. He bent down and scooped a handful of dirt. Fisting the earth angrily, he cursed. "Humans."

He closed his eyes, reining in years of caged fury. Now was not the time to do something hasty or lose his head and waste his efforts to bring back the true king, his king, King Drest. Soul-damaging sacrifices beyond redemption had been put in place. Hell, even his sister had paid the price with her life. Marcus had tried to save her by sending her to England and far away from Drest. She had been at court and awaited a perfect suitor. She was supposed to marry a nobleman, someone to protect her. With their parents long gone and cold in the grave, Marcus had been entrusted to look after his sister and he had failed.

Driven to spilling dragon blood on holy ground, he'd gone as far as betraying his cousin and one time friend, James Douglas. Although he had underestimated James's strength, Marcus did outwit him. At times, it had been daunting keeping his dragon a secret from James since they had been so close, but it paid off at the end. Marcus held no regrets for pushing James to the point where the Black Douglas had spilled his cousin's blood on holy ground, awakening the king unknowingly. Marcus was willing to give his life in order for Drest to live.

Even though he hadn't lived through the battle centuries ago, he had lived through the aftermath. Demons plagued the Stewart family, starting back when MacAlpin had slaughtered his great-grandfather. Revenge and hatred toward humans grew stronger and stronger through each generation, and now Marcus was going to end the suffering.

He opened his hand allowing the dirt to flow over his fingertips. Aye, he would indeed end the suffering of his people. Humans didn't deserve to live happily while his kind mourned. A sinister grin crept across his stone-cold face as he watched the dirt fall to the ground. Drest was here below the earth; he felt his king scratching to resurface and reclaim his land. And Marcus was here to make sure his king wasn't disappointed.

Heavy footsteps brought Marcus's attention to the Creeper in front of him.

"My laird, I caught the female trying to escape." The black-clad Creeper threw Kate to the ground.

Marcus stood and looked down at Kate crossly. "I admire yer will, lass, but there's no escaping."

"Ye can no' keep me here."

Marcus bent down to her level. "Ye will serve me," he seethed into her ear. "Ye will serve me king and heal him back to life."

"I will do no such thing," Kate bit back.

Marcus raised his hand and slapped her across the face. "Ye will serve me king." He raised his hand again but held back when he saw the lass cover her face in anticipation of another blow.

"Good. I knew ye'd see it me way."

~

*J*t took all of Kate's might to gain her footing and stand. She knew it had been a mistake to try and run away, but the opportunity arose, the men were distracted, and the temptation to run took over. On horseback, she and Aela had ridden through the glen, only to have their horse trip over a root and throw them from its back. The women instantly gained their footing and took off, running in opposite directions because their lives depended on it. With her hands free Kate thought she had a chance to get away, but alas she wasn't fast enough. One of Marcus's men was on her before she knew what was happening. The cold, black-clad Creeper tackled her to the ground, capturing her hands before she could attack the bastard with her light.

Now she stood out of breath and out of hope as her cheek swelled. She watched with suspicious eyes as she strained to hear what Marcus was discussing with the man. But it was of no use. They talked low and as soon as they saw her looking, they turned their backs. Inwardly she smiled; she might have been caught, but she still held her amulet and the blood they needed.

Kate took a step back as the Creeper advanced on her and grabbed her arm. Kate struggled against the sting of his hold and in return her captor elbowed her in the face, causing her vision to blur and her legs to buckle. In one swift motion the Creeper hoisted her up onto his shoulder. At this moment Kate realized that no matter how much she fought, she would fail. It was no use; Marcus was going to prevail.

She blinked back the fog as a tent bounced into view. Praying, she willed her legs to move, to kick, to do something, but the fog was too thick. Her eyes weakly shut and her body went limp.

A few hours passed and Kate sluggishly opened her eyes. An orange glow illuminated her surroundings and the heat from a nearby fire warmed her body. As her vision cleared, she came to realized she was inside a tent. Panicked, Kate tried to sit up but was restricted. The sound of chains clinking together drove her will to escape further as she thrashed her arms about, struggling to break free.

A low sinister snicker rumbled from the corner of the tent. Quickly, Kate looked toward the noise and swallowed hard. She wasn't alone.

"Nay need to struggle, rabbit. Laird Marcus put me in charge of ye and ye be going nowhere," the man in the shadows seethed.

The voice was unrecognizable and sent a chill racing down her spine.

The wind from outside howled and blew the tent, rippling its fabric. The fire flickered and danced to an eerie sway. Still weak from the blow to her head, Kate lay back down. Tears silently streamed down her cheeks, wetting her hair. How was she going to get out of this mess?

A chair creaked and the air thickened around her. The man from the shadows revealed himself as he hovered over her, smiling a sickening grin. Pure horror ripped through her...it was the man from the tavern with the black smoke.

"Ah now, rabbit, I thought ye'd be happier than that to see me." He looked down at Kate and studied her.

"Dinnae touch me, ye bastard," she spat.

"Now, let's no' get hasty. Me name is Tavish."

"I dinnae care who ye are, just dinnae touch me."

Tavish sat down on the cot beside her and slowly moved her dress up her legs, stopping at the knee. He looked at her as if she was the game he had proudly hunted and now wanted to devour.

Kate's heart raced and thumped against her ribcage. "Please," she whispered. "Dinnae touch me."

"Ye see, rabbit, that's going to be a problem. Ye have something we want and I was sent here to retrieve it." Tavish slid her dress up higher, to mid-thigh. He trailed his rough hand down her leg and back up again.

With every touch Kate's skin prickled in vile disgust. Bile rose in the back of her throat as she thought about what this monster had in store for her if she didn't give him the amulet. Regardless, if she gave the blood to him or not, he most certainly would have his way with her. She gasped as Tavish's hand slid farther up her thigh to her stocking and rolled the woolen fabric down. She needed her hands free.

Kate swallowed hard. "Do ye touch all the lasses like this?"

Tavish paused. "What do ye mean?"

"Ye have a soft touch. If I'm guessing right, ye must have the lasses melting beneath yer hand." Kate had never seduced a man before, nor did she know if she was saying the words a man wanted to hear. The drive to escape pushed her beyond comfort; it was pure survival instinct motivating her, driving her to do whatever it took to be free.

Tavish was clearly taken aback by her comment. "Rabbit, if ye think ye can oot wit me ye be mistaken." Roughly he grabbed her other leg and tore her stocking off.

Kate gasped. "Please, it doesn't have to be like this. I know I can no' escape and even if I tried, a wee lass like meself can no' make it through the dangers of the Highlands. I know what ye want and I'm willing to give it if ye release me hands."

Tavish looked her up and down with the devil in his eyes. "Why should I trust ye?"

"Ye dinnae. But I suspect ye want to be in Laird Marcus's good favor, aye?"

"Aye."

"I'll give ye want ye want. Then ye can prove to Marcus ye are a trusted and loyal warrior and I can experience yer ways in pleasuring a lass." Kate fought hard to keep her composure and sound convincing. She rubbed her bare leg against him and grinned.

Tavish leaned in and nuzzled her neck, taking in a deep breath. "Ye be intoxicating."

The bile rose farther up her throat as she tamped down the urge to vomit. Kate arched her back. "Let me show ye how intoxicating I can be," she whispered in his ear.

In one fluid motion, Kate heard the restraints snap and broken chain-links fell to the ground. Her hands were free. Fear reared its ugly head as she was trapped underneath the heaviness of Tavish's body. With the way his arousal pressed into her stomach, she had to pull herself together and break free fast.

Her eyes widened when Tavish bent down to kiss her. She turned her head from the rankness of his breath. Inwardly she counted to three then lifted her knee, connecting to his prized jewels. Howling in pain, Tavish rolled off her and onto the floor, clenching his ballocks. "Ye wench!"

With haste Kate stood and kicked him in his already aching cock. 'I told ye no' to touch me," she bit back.

As she ran to the opening of the tent she spotted his sword resting against the chair. Thinking it was silly to waste her time on trying to pick up a heavy sword, she tried anyway. To her surprise it was light and fit nicely in her hands. She took the sword and left the tent.

Outside she saw that night had fallen over the auld kingdom, making her question how long she'd been unconscious. A few tents were littered about and no one was outside. Hurriedly, she ran over to a broken down stone wall and hid herself behind it. She couldn't stay here for much longer. Tavish would be hot on her heels before long. A crunching sound came from off in the distance, causing her to hug the wall closer. She peeked over the side and was relieved to see five horses; one was munching on grass.

Kate took in a deep breath and gathered up her courage to make a run for it to the horse.

"Rabbit, ye better run." Tavish burst out of the tent, stumbling.

Kate froze with panic; her time was up. She palmed the hilt of the sword and sent a prayer up to heaven. She had to make it to a horse before that monster found her, because if he caught her, surely he would make her pay for her deceit. Taking in a shaky breath, Kate peeked over the wall again, searching for another landmark to hide behind that was closer to the horses. They were still too far away to reach and Tavish would catch her in no time. To her dismay there was nothing between her and the horses. She cursed silently.

Kate gathered up all the courage and fight she had left, regardless of how badly her body protested. Her muscles ached and her bare feet were bleeding and cut from the sharp rocks on the ground, but that would be the least of her pain if Tavish caught her. She had made it this far; there was no going back.

Tamping down her fears, she ran toward her goal, never chancing a look behind. Heavy footsteps fell behind her, only a breath away, as she felt his hands wisp past her hair. The sword slipped from her grasp and she dropped it. Without the weight of the sword holding her down, she pumped her legs faster. The horses seemed as if they were moving farther and farther away.

Just a few more strides, it was all she needed, until Tavish lunged forward and grabbed her legs. The amulet flew from the top of her dress and spun in the air in slow motion as she tried desperately to grab it before it hit the ground. With full force, the amulet escaped her grasp and fell in front of her. The locket cracked and dark red blood leaked out and was quickly absorbed into the earth.

"Nay!" Kate yelled.

Immediately Tavish rolled her over onto her back, oblivious to what had taken place. "Ye should have run faster, rabbit," he seethed.

Kate screamed and kicked with every fiber of her being, but it was pointless. Tavish covered her mouth and pushed her skirts up around her waist. Tears streamed down her face as she clamped her teeth round his hand, biting through skin.

Tavish wailed in pain and struck her across the face. Blood poured from her lips. Not only had she been captured again, but the blood that would awaken King Drest had seeped into holy ground.

21

*D*ue to the speed with which the warriors took flight, and with Hawk locked onto Kate's scent, the dragons were able to track her to the auld kingdom of Govan without any delays, although there was an uncomfortable silence, and a few hard glances passed between Hawk and Magnus. Hawk couldn't mask having bedding Magnus's daughter, and it was clear he had not only disrespected the warrior, but also soured Kate's good name.

Hawk had never been told about the principles of a Dragonkine mate. Aye, he was thoroughly attracted to Kate, but her being his mate hadn't crossed his mind. Perhaps if he hadn't been busy pushing her away, he would have known, but then again would it have mattered? He had sought the answer ever since he left Helmfirth in search of her. Indeed he couldn't refuse the lass and was happy that he'd taken her to bed, especially now, since he was able to track her scent.

One thing held true; once a Kine bedded their mate, something magical took place. No matter where their mate might be, a dragon always knew where to find his female. Hawk could feel it now, the closer he got to her. Every fiber of Kate pulsed through him like a rhythmic connection he couldn't deny; so to say he regretted taking what Kate had been willing to give was far from the truth.

The three dragons landed within the glen and shifted back into their Highlander form, laying low and on guard as they stayed out of sight of Marcus and his Creepers. Impatient and annoyed, Hawk worked his jaw, reeling in his anger as he hid behind an auld yew tree, feeling helpless. With a keen eye he searched the grounds for any signs of Kate. Alarmingly silent.

Hawk closed his eyes and honed in on her, breathing her into his body. Fury hung on by a thread as he sensed she was in danger. Her fear ripped through him like a lightning bolt. Immediately he opened his eyes and growled low and deep as his dragon paced back and forth, clawing to be released. Sweat glistened on his skin and scales appeared. The thread frayed and Hawk stepped out of the shadows.

As if Magnus could feel the shift in the air he motioned for the red-headed warrior to stand down as Magnus crouched behind the thick brush.

Hawk paused and pinned Magnus with a puzzled glare.

Magnus mouthed, *No' now*, then pointed to a Creeper walking past a tent.

With much restraint, Hawk resumed his position behind the yew tree. Time seemed to be wasting away the more he remained still. With every pulse he felt Kate's fear grow stronger. She needed his help and all he could do was stay hidden and do nothing. God's teeth, he was going to go daft if they didn't do something quick.

The air between the two Highlanders stilled as they heard a rustle through the bush. With both men on high guard they hadn't recognized their own kin. After taking a closer look at the auld kingdom, Rory returned with news. He motioned for the men to come closer.

"There's seven Creepers. Tavish and Kate are in that tent," Rory whispered and pointed to a gold tent.

*H*awk straightened when he heard Kate's name. Now he knew exactly what he was dealing with and there would be no more wasting time. He strode past the men and was headed in the direction of the tent when he felt a hand grab his arm and stop him.

He turned and looked at the culprit who dared lay a hand on him. He met Magnus's blazing eyes. "I promised her mother I'd return our daughter unharmed," he stated sternly.

"With all due respect, release me and I shall retrieve yer daughter," Hawk commanded.

"Dinnae lose yer head." Magnus released Hawk's arm.

A bloodcurdling shriek echoed in the dead of the night. Hawk froze, it was Kate.

Like hell nipping at his heels, Hawk ran toward the scream, shedding his human skin. With each stride he succumbed to his dragon, allowing the fury to take over. Red scales rippled down his back, wings unfolded and straightened for flight. With two powerful pumps of his wings he took to the sky and straight to Kate.

As she came into view, Hawk bared his teeth when he saw the creature that had attacked him and his home, assaulting Kate. She was fighting for her life. Pure rage boiled in his blood and his dragon craved revenge. Hawk honed in on Tavish and swooped down. Long, sharp talons pierced through Tavish's back, sinking in until the daggers reached bone. Hawk snarled in pleasure when the fool shrieked out in pain. The surprise of it all left Tavish flailing about as Hawk plucked Tavish off Kate like one of his raptors going in for the kill.

Hawk tossed his enemy up in the air and caught him by the neck, snapping it intently in his mouth. Although the kill had been too fast for what the creature deserved, Hawk had to see to his mate. Throwing the lifeless body to the ground, Hawk landed by Kate and shifted to the man she would recognize.

"Did he hurt ye?" Hawk went to her quickly, cupping her face. Tears streamed down her dirty cheeks and he wiped the blood from her bottom lip. The lump in his chest shattered when he looked into her hazel eyes. "My God Kate, the bastard hurt ye did he no'?"

Kate shook her head.

The weight he had been holding on his shoulders crashed to the ground and he pulled her into a tight embrace. "I'm so sorry," he whispered against her hair and kissed the top of her head.

"Hawk, we have a serious problem," Kate warned.

"I know, lass. I should have—"

"Nay." She pulled away from him. "Dragon blood has been spilled on holy ground." She pointed to her cracked amulet.

Hawk stepped in front of her and bent down, rubbing his hand through the dirt. Deep cracks separated the ground like a spider's web and grew deeper. The earth shook and rumbled. Hawk took a step back in shock.

At that instant Magnus and Rory landed, still in dragon form. Hawk turned to the dragons. "We have a problem. Drest lives."

Right then the whole kingdom of Govan came alive. Old earth shook and fell into the deep cracks. The trembling grew more violent as the menace ripped and clawed its way out from the underworld. Flames licked up through the cracks, setting fire to the grounds.

Marcus and his Creepers came running from their tents, trying to keep their balance against the shaking earth. As soon as the Creepers made eye contact, they charged Magnus and Rory, and the battle began.

Hawk grabbed Kate's hand. "We have to get oot of here, now!"

Kate looked at the flames then to Hawk and nodded.

Because it was second nature to Hawk, he shifted. "Have ye ever flown with a dragon before?"

Wide-eyed, Kate looked at the red beast. The dragon lowered his head. "Dinnae be afraid. I'd take my own life before I'd hurt ye."

Kate took a step back. "How is it that I can hear ye when yer lips do no' move?"

"'Tis through mind speak that we can talk and hear each other."

"Amazing," she said without moving her lips. Kate walked closer to the dragon and ran her hands down his neck in amazement.

Hawk leaned into her touch and wished they had more time, for his dragon craved more of her soft touch. "Lass, we need to leave." He lowered his wing and without hesitation his mate climbed her way up between his shoulder blades. With Kate nestled upon his back, he took three long strides, gaining momentum for flight when the ground split beneath him and his back foot slipped into the cracked earth. The crack widened and crumbled away. Frantically flapping his wings, he fought against gravity threatening to pull them down into the blazing firestorm below. "Hang on!" Hawk growled. Without the momentum he needed to take flight it was going to be difficult to take to the sky and fly them out of here.

With all his might he pumped his massive wings, cautious not to knock Kate off. He hadn't come this far to lose her. No matter how hard he pushed he couldn't gain the upper hand. It was like he was being sucked down by some powerful force and he slid deeper into the crack. His heart stopped when Kate's grip slip from his spikes. He couldn't risk her life anymore. At least if she was on land Magnus could get her out of this fiery inferno.

"Kate, me strength is fading fast. Ye need to get to yer da and get out of here."

"Nay, I won't leave ye."

"Ye must. Ye're going to climb up my neck and get on land."

"Hawk, I—"

"There's no time to argue. Do it now!"

⁓

*W*ith haste, Kate crawled up his neck and reached land. She spun back to help Hawk when right before her a giant flame blazed toward the sky, engulfing Hawk in its fury. Kate hid her face behind her arms from the blaze, its heat singeing her skin. As quickly as the blaze came it disappeared. "Nay, Hawk!" Kate ran to the edge of the crack and fell to her knees, looking over the edge. Hawk was gone. "Hawk! Nay!"

Hot searing air blew up from the firestorm below, knocking Kate backwards. White smoke swirled up and hovered over the land. Right in front of her eyes the smoke wisped about and transformed into a human form. Flashes of light flickered through the night sky and the earth became eerily silent.

Black wings as dark as ravens unfolded and revealed a man of noble stature. Marcus and the Creepers ceased to battle and fell on their knees in front of their king. Kate scooted back from the sight, and was halted when her back bumped against something hard. She looked behind her. Gaping up at the giant scaled leg, she traced the leg upward with her eyes to the beast's chest then head. Brown eyes bore down on her, casting a sense of auld-worldly wisdom.

"Da?" Kate questioned, in awe of the massive beast.

"Aye, Kate, we must leave."

Kate shook her head. "Hawk, he's—" She didn't dare complete her thought, for if she said it out loud then she had to believe it true that Hawk was dead.

Instantly Magnus scooped Kate up with his massive claws, ignoring her protesting body.

"Da, I can no' leave him. He can no' be dead."

"Lass, Hawk wouldn't want ye to stay in harm's way. He risked his life saving yers. Ye must leave now."

She ceased her protest as her father flapped his wings and took to the sky. The auld kingdom became smaller and smaller as Magnus flew them in the direction of Black Stone. Just before the last images of Govan disappeared, Kate reached her hand out. "Hawk," she whispered, "I love ye."

Before she knew it her body relaxed and her eyelids grew heavy. The fight was gone from her and she succumbed to sleep.

22

The morn shone bright over Black Stone on the Hill as the lady of the castle, Abigale Douglas, sat privately nursing her wee babe, Jamie. Anticipation swelled deep within her as she thought about the full day she'd planned for her daughters and a feisty gray colt.

A smile spread across her face as she took in the view. Clan Douglas was finishing breaking their fast in the great hall. Her husband and chieftain of the clan, James Douglas, sat at the head of the table, a pure statue of an honorable man, dominating, and extremely sexy. Abigale considered herself one lucky lass to be his wife and the mother of his child. He was a good man and cared for his clan like family. A smile escaped her when James smiled and winked at her from across the room. Indeed, a very lucky lass.

Next to her husband, another honorable man, Conall, sat beside his very pregnant wife and Abigale's best friend, Effie. Over the course of the morning feast, Conall's hands didn't leave Effie's swollen belly. Abigale could see the love for each other in their eyes. And then there were her two beautiful adopted daughters, Annis and Flora, sitting with Alice, teaching the girls proper table etiquette. Aye, Lady Douglas couldn't be happier.

A small fuss coming from her lap drew Abigale's attention to wee Jamie. "Och, my sweet lass, ye must be full." She beamed at the bundled babe while she tied the front of her dress.

"I think Jamie misses her da." From out of nowhere James appeared, bent down and kissed his wife ever so gently on the forehead.

Abigale handed the babe to him. "I do believe she fancies her da." The smile on her face widened when she looked at the perfect picture in front of her—her husband making silly faces at Jamie while the babe laughed and kicked her legs for joy. Abigale stood and brushed her fingers through Jamie's black hair, marveling in its fullness.

"I sent Neven to fetch the colt for Annis," James said.

"Verra good. She'll be so excited to finally work with him."

They walked together past the great hall and out the double doors leading to the courtyard. Before the doors closed the soft pitter-patter of footsteps pranced behind them.

"Annis, are ye ready for yer first lesson, lass?" James asked.

The blonde child nodded excitedly.

From the day Abigale had rescued the sisters, Annis hadn't said a word. Flora did most of the speaking for her, but Abigale had caught on quite quickly and developed her own way of communicating with the child.

Abigale smiled at Annis and held her hand as the Douglases made their way to a vacant field where they met Neven. On one end of a rope the feisty colt bucked, kicking up his hooves, and on the other end Neven held on, trying hard not to get kicked.

As James approached the lad he laughed. "Och, laddie, looks like the wee colt is frisky this morn."

Frustrated, Neven huffed. "He be just like his da."

Abigale and James laughed. The colt was indeed the spitting image of Fergus, attitude and all. Fergus had been Abigale's warhorse, given to her by her da on one of his visits to the nunnery. Fergus was more than just a horse; he was her friend. It had devastated Abigale when Fergus died as a result of her reckless behavior.

Once she found out that James's mare was pregnant with Fergus's colt, she couldn't have been more pleased.

As soon as the colt saw Annis, his ears stood at attention and he nickered.

Without hesitation, Annis took the rope and walked toward the colt. His head was held high as he stood staring at the child as if he was deciding whether to take off running. Fearless, Annis reached for his nose and gave it a rub. As trust flourished between them, the colt lowered his head, rubbing against the child.

She ran her fingers through the colt's coarse white mane and marveled at the deep gray dapples that shined under the sun's rays. Even though she couldn't speak, the spark in Annis's blue eyes spoke more than words to Abigale. She knew exactly how the child was feeling because she had felt the same way about Fergus.

A tear rolled down Abigale's cheek, and she brushed it away nonchalantly before her husband noticed. She cleared her throat as she watched Annis lead the colt to an open area, preparing him to be led. Abigale started to go to the pair, but stopped when James held her back. Questioningly, Abigale looked at him with furrowed brows.

"Bel ange, let Annis be. Let her learn on her own. Watch, she's a natural." In one arm he held wee Jamie and the other he wrapped around his wife's shoulders, comforting her.

"I suppose ye're right."

James peered down at Abigale with a raised brow in surprise.

"Och, James Douglas, ye be right," she mockingly teased, tickling her daughter's feet.

At that moment Effie and Conall joined the Douglases as they watched Annis leading her colt around in a big circle.

"She's verra good with horses," Conall said as he greeted Abigale with a kiss on the cheek.

"Aye. To be that young and have no fear, 'tis fairly impressive," James agreed.

Abigale turned to her husband. "I've been thinking."

At that moment both men let out an irritated huff.

Effie elbowed Conall in the stomach. "What? Just because a woman has been thinking it does no' mean 'tis a bad thing."

"Nay, but it usually means there's work involved for the man when their lady conjures a daft idea in her head," James barked.

Annoyed, Abigale braced her hands on her hips and held them there with a tight grip before she lost her composure and slugged James for the rude comment. "For yer information, James Douglas, this has nothin' to do with ye over-exerting yerself."

"Och then, oot wit' it. What could possibly be so important?" James rolled his eyes.

"Flora." Abigale stiffened her chin. "She'll be of age soon and we need to start looking for a proper suitor for her."

Abigale watched James's Adam's apple slide up and down his throat, as he swallowed hard. "A suitor?"

"Aye."

"Does Flora know aboot yer brilliant idea?"

"Aye. She confided in me aboot such and I think 'tis time we start the process."

A small cough coming from Neven interrupted the conversation.

"Are ye alright lad?" James queried. He had taken Neven in as his squire after both the boy's parents were murdered a few years back, and they shared a father/son love even though James wasn't his kin.

Neven cleared his throat and his voice hitched an octave higher. "Aye, I'm fine."

Bringing James's attention back to the subject at hand, Abigale continued. "I think we should send word to all neighboring clans and host a gathering in Flora's honor."

Effie went to James and reached her arms out, offering to hold Jamie. "A coming of age celebration, what a fantastic idea. Oh, Alice could make her a stunning dress." She took the babe in her arms, beaming in delight.

Excitement rose and billowed over as ideas flooded through Abigale. "Aye, and we could hold the gathering in the great hall and —"

"Wait, I do no' approve of this daft idea," James thundered. "There's no rush in finding a suitor for Flora."

Abigale sauntered up to him, luring him in with her seductive blue eyes and calming the beast. She caressed his forearm softly with her fingertips. "Love, I'm no' planning a wedding. I know ye well. No lad will never be good enough for yer Flora, but she's growing up. We should help her while she still wants our help."

James grumbled something inaudible beneath his breath.

"Ye know I'm right aboot this."

James huffed, "Aye."

Standing on her tiptoes and barely reaching her husband's lips, she kissed him. "This will make her verra happy."

"Aye, but it's breaking me heart. I love that lass like she's me own blood."

"I know ye do, love," Abigale smiled. "That's why we must do this for her."

The air around them shifted. At that moment a winged shadow circled the ground. The familiar winds pricked Abigale's skin as she looked to the sky. Two very large dragons circled above and Lady Douglas smiled. "Magnus and Rory are home."

Conall ran over to Annis and gained control of the colt before the dragons landed and it spooked from the thunderous landing. James handed wee Jamie to Abigale and strode over to the dragons, feeling a sense of urgency.

By the time James reached the dragons, they had already shifted to their Highlander form. "Magnus, what happened?" he asked when he saw the warrior holding an unconscious woman in his arms.

"'Tis no' good, laddie. Drest is awake."

The gashes on their soot-covered bodies told of a grim story that had turned tragic.

"Abigale!" James called over his shoulder. "We need ye, lass."

Abigale stood frozen. There was a woman in Magnus's arms and they needed her assistance; this could not be good.

"I'll take Annis and Jamie back home and check on Flora. Ye are needed." Effie nodded her chin to the dragons. "Do no' fash yerself. I'll take care of the children."

Speechless, Abigale took off toward her husband and abruptly stopped when the lass came into view. "Sister Kate?"

"'Tis a long story, my lady. She's me daughter. I had to put her into a magic induced sleep. Kate's no' wounded physically, but I'm afraid her heart is."

Abigale brushed away Kate's hair from her face and felt for fever.

"What happened?" James barked out.

Rory looked to the ground and shook his head as if he mourned a loved one.

James looked at Rory with a vigorous glare, then to Magnus.

Before James could unleash his wrath, Magnus stepped forward. "Hawk is...dead. Kate witnessed everything and..." His voice broke, the words hitching in his throat.

By their grim faces, Abigale could sense that there was more to it than that. She feared that Kate had lost a love. True to her natural instincts, Abigale took charge. She placed her hand on James's shoulder, soothing some of his tension away. "James, there's an empty bedchamber across from Maggie's. Take Kate there and I'll be right behind ye."

"Aye." James scooped Kate into his arms and headed for the castle.

"Magnus, Rory, I'll come and check on yer wounds after I tend to Kate."

"Nay, lass." Magnus placed his hands on her shoulders and bore into her eyes as he towered over her. "Make sure me daughter is well. She's in shock."

"I will." Abigale gave her best sympathetic smile, but deep down she knew Kate may very well never recover from this tragedy. Abigale had been there, right where Kate was suffering now. She had experienced the empty numbness before. The loneliness never really went away as she recalled the memory of losing Fergus.

As she made her way to the castle, right then and there she

prayed for Sister Kate, for a broken heart was a daunting mend; a wound that never fully healed.

~

*A*lice brought the naked warriors some clothes, the Guardians sat in the solar as James called for a meeting. Magnus retold the events that had taken place over the last few weeks—how he and Rory had been led to Govan and the awakening of King Drest. The mention of his name brought an eerie silence over the room.

James sat in deep thought, rubbing his chin as he took in the information. Drest was alive, and it was not good. He had known that eventually this day would come, however he'd hoped it would not be this soon. King Drest would demand an audience from the Kine and there would be no denying the king. When the alpha called, the dragons answered.

How was he going to protect the humans he loved from the wrath of Drest? Because it would be a cold day in hell before he would join the king. An image of young Jamie happily, freely running through the heather crept into his thoughts. Nay, he would never join Drest and allow his family to become the dragon king's slaves.

On the other hand, he would have to live with the blood of his brethren on his hands if he refused to join the king. His men-at-arms, the fellow dragons he trusted, that had given their oath to Scotland, would follow him into a daunting battle that they could not win. That is if they would join him. What he needed was more dragons.

The discussion in the room distorted into muttering chatter as James fell farther into his troubled thoughts. His mood grew dark over the grim malice that had awoken. No matter what, his decision would be very difficult.

James peered around the room from warrior to warrior. They all held something close that they treasured. Conall, his best friend, had a human wife and a babe on the way. Magnus had a daughter and a female to protect. Rory yearned to be reunited with the true king and be out from underneath the human thumb. Caden was still a mystery, and now with the loss of Hawk—*Shite!* James scrubbed his hands down his face and took in a frustrated breath.

All at once the chatter grew louder as Conall and Rory broke out in an argument.

Conall stormed Rory, approaching him face-to-face. Cheeks reddened and nostrils flared. "Do ye have any idea as to what ye speak of?" Conall demanded.

Pushing his chest out, Rory met Conall's vigor. His dark gaze bore deep and dared Conall to disagree with him. "Aye, I do know what I speak of. I know I dinnae want a human king anymore."

"Ye only be a lad with boyish dreams, because no man would want Drest to rule," Conall seethed through gritted teeth.

"I be no lad—"

"Then stop thinking with yer cock long enough to realize we need humans to survive." Conall pushed his body against Rory's chest.

Before the warriors had a chance to further test their dragon mentality, Magnus stepped between the snarling, seething Highlanders. "Let's think aboot this for a moment, laddies. What if our king was right here in this room?"

The room fell silent. The fire in the hearth flickered and popped as the Highlanders held their gazes on James. Slowly, James lifted his head to meet eager eyes on him. At one moment he was ready to throw the men out on their arses, because he couldn't take the arguing anymore; the next minute he was rendered speechless.

Magnus pressed on. "James has brought us here together at Black Stone, welcomed us in like family. If any dragon has our best interest at heart, 'tis James."

Conall nodded and agreed.

Rory shouldered his way past Magnus and with angered strides he quit the room, slamming the door behind him. As he turned down the corridor, brooding in his rage, he nearly knocked Abigale down.

"Excuse me, my lady." He caught her before she stumbled to the ground.

"'Tis alright." She regained her balance. "Ye be well, Rory?"

"Aye, I need some fresh air." With that, he continued down the corridor and disappeared from Abigale's sight.

Shaking her head, she dismissed his odd behavior and made her way to the solar to give notice about Kate.

Lightly she knocked on the door, knowing it was improper for her to disturb her husband in counsel, but she had to inform Magnus about the condition of his daughter. James would understand, for if it was one of his daughters in the same situation, he would want to know her progress as soon as possible.

"Come in," James barked out in frustration.

The air in the room was full of tension and something else. Dread. With all eyes on her, Abigale swallowed hard as Magnus approached her eagerly. "Please pardon me interruption. I come to tell ye that Kate fares well. Her wounds do no' run skin deep, but soul deep. She needs rest and time to heal." Abigale took Magnus's shaking hands in hers. "Knowing Kate, she's strong and she will be alright."

"Aye, we shall see, lass. She witnessed her mate's death. A broken heart is a hard wound to mend." Magnus's gaze fell to the ground as he quit the solar.

Abigale fixed her eyes on James as he poured two tankards of wine. Without a word, he handed one to his beautiful wife, then took a seat in a chair big enough for a king in front of the window overlooking rolling green hills. White as freshly fallen snow, sheep dotted the land. A strong wind from the east blew through the tall grass, dancing to nature's harmony. A tranquil sight, indeed. Today, he wished to be a dragon, flying high over Black Hill, leaving behind this dire situation. He could scoop his family up and fly them all far away where no one, not even a king, could find them.

When he married Abigale, he made an oath to King Robert the Bruce to protect his daughter at all costs. He made an oath to Scotland to protect her from absolute destruction from any evil tyrant that may dare test their power over her. King Robert had upheld his vow and defeated the English armies who threatened to seize his lands. Now it was time for James to do the same, yet on a larger scale. He was going up against a dragon: his own kind.

Warm, gentle hands massaged his tense shoulders, soothing him like nothing else. The woman knew all the right places to touch. James leaned back into Abigale's hands and closed his eyes. She traveled her hands up his neck to his head, raking her nails against his scalp through his long black hair. "God's teeth woman, yer hands are magic," he sighed.

Abigale smiled and deepened the pressure. "Ye look as if ye be troubled, my love."

"Aye."

"Do ye need to talk aboot it?"

James didn't answer her right away, for he didn't desire to discuss Kine business with her. However, knowing his wife's prescience, he had no choice in the matter. Furthermore, it was time Abigale knew of the menace that had awakened. He hadn't fully explained to her about the ongoing quakes. Most of the time the shakes were so trivial that only a Dragonkine could feel the earth quiver in anticipation of Drest's arrival.

The warrior was only protecting his wife. Abigale had been pregnant at the time, and informing her about the beast below would have caused her stress and harmed their unborn babe. Now, with all danger aside, he had to tell her everything...well, almost everything.

"Bel ange, come sit." He patted his war-hardened hands on his thighs.

Abigale did exactly as she was told and sat across his lap, peering with concern into his deep amber eyes. "James, ye be scaring me. What troubles ye?"

After placing the tankard on the ground, he took his wife's hands in his. They were so delicate compared to his. "I have no' been honest wit' ye."

Abigale froze, her blue eyes widening as she tried to calm her rapid beating heart.

James brushed back a strand of auburn hair that had come loose from her long thick braid. "The quakes ye have been feeling are much more to worry about than I have led ye to believe." He gave her hand a squeeze before he carried on. "Remember me telling ye about Drest and what happened to Dragonkine?"

"Aye."

"Drest has risen. He will want all dragons on his side to seek his vengeance against humans."

Abigale sat silent as she took in this information. She'd had a sneaking suspicion that the quakes were indeed something to worry about, yet she'd kept her suspicions to herself.

"I made an oath to yer father to protect ye from this, but I have to protect me Kine as well. Magnus and Conall believe I should be king and fight Drest. I fear if I make the wrong decision I will fail greatly. Not only will I fail ye, I will fail my Kine."

Hearing her husband proclaim his weaknesses shattered Abigale's heart. To see the mighty Black Douglas defeated before he'd had the chance to fight was not sitting well with her. She also had the faith in her husband, knowing this man had conquered and fought his way through Scotland, serving her father as a loyal knight. There was nothing the Black Douglas couldn't defeat. She knew wholeheartedly that her husband would move mountains to protect his own.

Abigale took James's head in her hands and held his amber stare. "James Douglas, ye be one fine man. It shows on every face here at Black Stone, and the Kine have the utmost respect for ye. They trust ye."

"How can I allow my men to follow me into a war we can no' win? Drest has seven death dragons and Marcus as allies. And possibly Rory. We are greatly outnumbered."

"Do ye trust me?"

'Twas an odd question coming from Abigale. Of course he trusted her. "Aye."

"Then trust in me when I say ye're a leader. Ye will lead yer men into victory because they know ye're a man of honor. A man who will fight to the death to protect the ones he loves. A man they will want to follow to defeat a tyrant dragon. Yer men chose ye, James, because of what ye stand for."

"But I am no king."

"I beg to differ and so do Magnus and Conall."

James sat and thought about his wife's words of wisdom. Where had his warrior mentality gone? Since settling down and staying off the battlefield, he had been lying low, playing it safe, leaving the fighting to someone else in order to protect his family. Had family life turned him soft?

Despite all his efforts to create a secluded place for his family, the enemy had found him. Neither Highlander nor dragon would ever roll over and allow the enemy to conquer their lair. It wasn't in their blood to fall to weakness. But ye add a woman and children into his life...by fair means or foul a dragon protects his own.

"Bel ange, ye are me strength." He kissed his wife. "Ye'll make one fine queen."

Abigale looked down into her lap.

James became alarmed. "What be on yer mind, lass?" He could feel her distress running through his veins like a stream. When she didn't answer right away he lifted her chin with his finger, bringing her eyes to his. "Abigale," he said sternly.

"I know 'tis no' a good time to tell ye, but I can no longer keep a secret." A tear trickled down her cheek.

"Please tell me, Abigale. Ye know I can no' stand to see ye cry."

"I'm wit' child." That one lonely tear was joined by several others.

James sat stunned at first, then beamed at his wife. Another babe on the way. He couldn't be happier.

"Are ye sure? It's so soon after Jamie's birth."

Abigale wiped the tears from her face with the back of her hand and took a deep breath. "I thought so too, but Alice is most certain that I'm wit' child. Perhaps eight weeks."

James took his beautiful wife in his arms and hugged her tightly, kissing her thoroughly. More than ever he was determined to fight Drest and send the bastard back where he came from. No one dared to pose a threat to his family without a bloody battle. James's dragon stirred as if a fire had been lit.

A knock on the solar door intruded into his thoughts. He broke the kiss long enough to demand the intruder go away.

"But my laird, ye must come down to the great hall. 'Tis of great urgency," Neven called out.

"That lad has the most impeccable timing," James jested as he kissed his wife one last time. As he quit the room he felt as if something was missing. He peeked back in and watched Abigale wipe more tears away. "Bel ange, ye coming wit' me?"

Abigale smiled through the tears. "I'll be down in a moment."

"Aye." James looked her up and down with his smoldering amber gaze. "Dinnae keep me waiting, lass. I want those hands upon me body again." He winked.

Abigale giggled. "I shall no' keep the Black Douglas waiting long."

James smiled and left the solar.

With long, authoritative strides, he made it to the end of the corridor and took the steps leading down into the great hall. Midway down the stairs he paused as he viewed at least three chieftains from three different clans sitting at his table as Alice served them ale, bread, and cheese. Conall, Magnus, and Caden stood on alert, watching every move the men made. What in the devil was going on?

A tingle jolted through James as he reached the great hall. All the hairs on the back of his neck stood, and the sensation intensified the closer he got to the men. There was something amiss here, yet he couldn't quite put his claw on it. He sensed his own kind in spite of the humans in his hall.

Everyone stood and bowed their heads when James entered. His brows furrowed together. "What brings ye here?"

The first man to step forward was big and burly. He looked to be older and was battle-worn with a scar running down his left cheek. "Me name is Sir Symon MacBain, Laird of the North, at yer service, my laird."

James eyed the man for a while before he remembered him.

"Symon MacBain," he pondered. "Aye, ye battled at Bannockburn. Our allies to the North."

"Aye, a short, yet fine victory indeed," Symon commented.

"What brings ye here?"

"I come to offer aid in yer time of need. Not myself per se, but I have three verra stout sons that ye'll be quite impressed by."

"Symon, I can no' accept yer sons for this battle." Certainly, James could not allow humans to fight a Dragonkine war; they were helpless in the presence of a dragon. He would not be held responsible for their deaths. Furthermore, how did Symon know about his troubles?

Symon placed his thumb and index finger in his mouth and blew, sending out a shrill whistle. He glanced at James with a devilish gleam in his eyes. At that moment three young men, ranging from eight-and-ten to twenty-and-five, lined up side by side. They had their father's green eyes and brawn; their confidence escaped through every pore on their bodies.

"This be Duncan." He pointed to the lad who looked to be the eldest. "This be Graham and me youngest, Bane."

James stepped closer to the lads. There was something so very familiar, as if they were kin. All of his senses were pulled taut and on alert. He looked deeper into Duncan's green eyes, then to Graham, and then to Bane. As James studied Bane's eyes, a green swirl shined. Stunned, James staggered back. "What the devil, they're dragons?"

Symon's laugh bellowed through the hall. "Aye, me friend. There be more dragons than ye think."

At that moment two more chieftains stood alongside their sons, one who had twins.

James scrubbed a hand down his face, not believing his eyes. Conall joined James and slapped a hand on his shoulder. "Looks as though ye have yer dragons."

"Aye."

Indeed he had at least six young dragons to train and fight on their side.

"Conall, ye and Caden have yer hands full. These dragons will need to be trained."

Caden joined in as if he had appeared from out of nowhere. "I have no doubt we can train these hatchlings." Caden grinned and rubbed his hands together, eager to get started.

Magnus approached his brothers. "Where are we going to put them? I will no' forgo me chamber." He stood next to Conall, hands crossed over his chest.

"There be plenty of room in the south tower." Abigale slid between Caden and James and put her arm around her husband.

And in a blink of an eye, hope had been restored. He now had an army to train and hoped more would come.

23

The sun cast a golden orange hue over the moor. Tall brown grass danced back and forth in the cool breeze as Kate gathered her skirts in her hand and strolled through the thick vegetation. Her skin warmed and shimmered under the sun, her hair shining more honey brown than her normal darker color, and her smile beaming across her face as she twirled around and smiled at him.

Though the image was quite foggy, her emotions ran deep. She was happy, content—a feeling that in the real world she had yet to find. But here she was happy.

As if the scene morphed into another time and place, the feeling of contentment heated into desire. Hot, searing kisses left fiery trails down her slender neck and her breasts. Full soft lips captured her nipple and suckled until she felt the butterflies in the pit of her stomach stir. A most delicious flutter.

The weight of this man on top of her, settled between her legs, awoke her body time and time again. His scent, a mixture of spice and pine, she would never forget. His touch, strong and gentle, she would never feel again. His breath was hot against her lips; she would never taste another quite like him.

As her dream continued, her body began to heat. A tingling sensation swam through her veins relentlessly, the skin on her upper arms swirling into a million tiny continuous circles. Sweat beaded on her skin in an attempt to cool her. Even though her body lay still, inside she frantically tried to wake herself. As real as a heartbeat, his eyes were on her and she heard Hawk call her name. "Kate."

Startled, Kate sat straight up, her heart rapidly thumping against her ribcage. Her eyes darted around the room in search of Hawk. He was here; she could feel it. Just like every morn when she'd awoken, a flash of fire flickered through her vision as a reminder that her dragon was never coming back to her. He was gone.

Desperate to reclaim her lost dream, Kate lay back down and closed her eyes. Here in this beautiful delusion she could be one with him, soothing the ache in her chest. In the haze of her mind she felt alive once again and desperately clung to it like a babe to its mother.

As if a cruel joke had been played on her, a bright light shot through her bedchamber, piercing her eyelids. Kate moaned from the intrusion and pulled the sheet over her head.

"Mistress Kate," Alice scolded. "'Tis time ye be getting up." Alice flung the canopy curtain open and securely tied it back. "There be no hiding today, lass. Ye are needed in the kitchen."

Kate grumbled. "I'll be just a moment." A fortnight had passed since she arrived at Black Stone and her wounds still festered. She had grown accustomed to Alice's visits every morn, noon, and eve. It had been the same ritual day-to-day; pushing the furs from the windows in order to shed light, a meal, and smudging the chamber with burning sage to ward off the evil spirits that plagued her. Today, Kate's time spent grieving alone had ended. Alice would see to that.

"Lass, ye need to eat and drink." Alice wrinkled her nose. "And it be best if ye bathe before joining the lassies in the kitchen." The plump woman fetched two buckets of water that had been sitting next to a tub. Kate sighed when she saw the steam escape from the top of the buckets. Alice poured the water into a wooden tub and sprinkled lavender through the rolling mist. She then walked over to the foot of the bed and quickly opened Kate's trunk, pulling out a red dress, wool stockings, and soft leather shoes. Laying the garments on the bed, she said, "Lass, I'll leave ye to yer bath, but promise me ye'll eat."

Kate gave a weary smile. "I promise. Thank ye, Alice."

Before Alice left the bedchamber she turned back. "'Tis hard to lose a love, child, but dinnae feel guilty for living yer life. Ye have much to live for." With that, Alice shut the door behind her.

Kate flung the sheet from her body. Two weeks had passed since she'd left the bedchamber or her bed. It hurt too much to face the day without Hawk. There was no blanket warm enough to dispel the frigidity that chilled her.

She missed his voice, the smell of his skin, the touch of his hands. Even the uncomfortable silence he'd often created between them; she yearned to have those moments back. She missed his protectiveness, his vigor, his dominating ways. She missed Hawk. Kate closed her eyelids tightly as tears crept from the corner of her eyes. "Hawk, I miss you."

After there were no more tears to be shed. Kate sluggishly got to her feet. From across the room she eyed a chair sitting next to the window. As if the chair had sprouted hands, it pulled her to it. She rubbed her hand along the grain of the wood; it felt warm, as if someone had been sitting there. She studied it, looking behind it, sliding it to the left then to the right. She even picked it up to look underneath.

Shoving the chair to the floor, Kate ran to the window and looked to the sky in hopes of her dragon's return, in hopes of some sort of explanation of why she felt like Hawk had been here all along. She fisted her hands until her knuckles turned white. A disturbance coming from the gatehouse outside the bailey drew her attention and lit a spark of hope. Alas, a flock of birds scattered from a tree and flew into the sky. Sighing heavily, Kate hung her head when her beastie didn't appear. It was bad enough to be depressed but now delusional...for sure they were going to lock her up.

Funny enough, she cared naught. In fact, Kate would rather take her own life than to live with the constant ache in her chest. But she knew better than to succumb to the demons plaguing her mind. She walked away from the window and began to undress as she made her way to the tub. She lifted her shift over her head and threw it to the floor. Alice was right; she was in desperate need of a bath.

As Kate immersed herself in the steaming water, lavender petals collected at the surface, sending out a most relaxing scent. Taking a cloth that had been draped over the tub for her to use, she began to bathe herself clean. Starting from her wrist, light red swirls climbed her arms and shoulders. Delicately, she ran the cloth over the markings as if she was scared that if she rubbed too hard they might disappear. The markings were beautiful, and another reminder of how much she missed Hawk. Not only had he marked her skin, he'd also marked her soul.

Avoiding slipping back into her beautiful delusion, Kate leaned back and slid down into the water until her head was covered. This was her punishment for straying from the vows she had taken and falling into temptation. This grief she felt could very well turn into madness, because of the sins she had allowed in her life.

As the air escaped her lungs, her body felt like a rock sinking down into the bathwater. She opened her eyes and looked up through the water. The heat stung her eyes, but not enough for her to keep them shut. Perhaps she would stay here a wee bit longer until the air in her lungs escaped completely.

From where she lay, a shadow moved in front of her. Startled to not be alone, Kate quickly emerged from the water, frantically taking in much needed breaths. "Who's there?" She covered her breasts with her hands, turning around, sharply searching for the intruder. But there was nothing. "I'm truly going mad," she whispered.

~

*A*bigale, Alice and Effie, among others, were in the kitchen preparing the provisions for Flora's coming of age gathering —or as James would like to call it, a plain and simple gathering. Various meats roasted over the pits, sending out a most delightful aroma. Chopped carrots and neeps danced on the table as a kitchen maid sliced and diced them into a frenzy. Another maid pounded and kneaded her frustrations out on a slab of dough, soon to become a hot delicious morsel.

Today was Flora's big day, when she would finally be seen as a lady and not a child. She was bursting with excitement. Abigale had to giggle as Flora entered the kitchen, this time wearing a red dress: the third one she had shown her mother in the past hour.

"What aboot this one?" Flora asked as she twirled around.

"Och lass, ye look verra bonny," Alice said, looking up from stirring a mixture that was the beginning of her special oatcakes.

Abigale, who was washing tankards, stopped to look at her beautiful daughter. She approached the lass, wiping her hands on her apron. "I think red might be too bold a color for ye." She smiled as she smoothed Flora's long blonde hair over her shoulders. "The blue dress ye had on last really brings oot the color in yer eyes. What do ye think, Effie?"

"Aye." Effie, with her hand on her lower back, waddled over to the girl. "Now, what are ye going to do wit' your hair?"

"Oh, Aunt Effie, I dinnae know." Flora hung her shoulders and blew out a frustrated breath. "Seems as though I can no decide on what to wear, nor how I should wear me hair."

Neven came barreling through the kitchen and grabbed an apple from the fruit basket, coming to an abrupt stop as he eyed Flora. He sank his teeth into the plump apple, swallowing its sweet juices. "No matter what ye do, ye still have those lanky, skinny legs."

Alice gasped. "Why, ye wee bugger." Alice grabbed a wooden spoon and chased Neven out of the kitchen as he taunted Flora. "Spider legs, spider legs."

Crying, Flora fled to her bedchamber.

"I'll see to the lass," Effie offered. As she turned to leave the kitchen, she bumped into Kate. "I be terribly sorry, Kate. I didnae see ye there." In haste to catch up with Flora, Effie hadn't paid attention to her surroundings.

Kate stood and watched Effie waddle up the stairs after Flora. "What happened? Yer daughter looks distraught."

"Aye. Neven is forever teasing the poor lass. I think he likes her, but has a hard time showing it." She winked and moved back into the kitchen.

Kate gave her best attempt at a smile as she followed Abigale. "Alice said ye need me help. What can I do?"

"Aye, Flora's gathering is today and much work still needs to be done. Ye can start by chopping those onions over there." Abigale pointed to a bowl of round yellow onions. Kate began to chop, slicing a blade though the ridged skin.

"I'm happy to see ye're awake and fare well. I was worried aboot ye."

Kate hadn't realized how hard it was to pretend to be normal when she was still wounded deep inside. Knowing everyone had been worried about her, she had to put on a show and act as if she could cope with the loss of Hawk.

"Abigale, truly ye've no need to worry aboot me. Time heals all wounds, aye?" She felt like such a liar as those words passed over her lips. She didn't believe them one bit.

Abigale eyed her friend before she took up drying another tankard. "Certainly I'm happy that ye are here. I wish it was under different circumstances."

"I know. In the past few weeks I've learned so much aboot myself. I feel—"

"Lost," Abigale interrupted.

"Aye." Kate busied herself cutting the onions, one after another.

"I do no' claim to know how ye feel, but I too have lost. In time the pain does ease."

She knew Abigale was trying to help and didn't fault her for trying, but the fact remained that no amount of time could heal her; time could not erase the memory of Hawk, nor bring him back to her. "Hawk was a good man, Abigale. Ye would have liked him." She smiled when she thought of their time together, caught in the rain, throwing mud at each other, and at first how angry he had looked with dirt sliding down his face. "Even though he had his stubborn streaks, I still..."

Tears ran down her cheeks and her eyes stung. Her chest felt tight and she couldn't breathe as she thought about never seeing Hawk again. She thought she had been ready to face the world, to function normally without breaking down. However, the emotions still ran raw. The wounds were still too fresh.

Abigale went to her friend and took her in her arms, hugging her. "I know, Kate, it hurts."

Minutes passed as Abigale stayed, allowing Kate to cry and mourn for her loss. Breaking their embrace, Kate sniffed and wiped her eyes, taking in a deep breath.

Abigale rubbed her arms, giving her comfort. "Feel better?"

Kate smiled through the tears. "Blasted onions."

They both laughed out loud. Abigale took Kate's hand. "Let's go find Alice and see if she can help us get dressed for the gathering. I have a beautiful dark red dress ye would look stunning in."

"I...I..." Kate stuttered, not sure how it would be possible for her to attend the gathering. She had expected to stay in her bedchamber. Her breath hitched when she thought about all the people that would be there. She couldn't face that kind of reality yet. But one look at Abigale and she knew she could not turn her down.

"Kate." Abigale became serious. "Ye need this."

Her friend was right. She needed to give the real world a chance. It was time to move forward. "All right. I'll go."

24

*C*lan Douglas's great hall came alive to the tin whistle being piped through the room as neighboring clans and clan members danced in celebration. The feast had been plentiful, and widely enjoyed by all. The ale was now flowing freely and the rowdy reputation of the Highlands held true, but all in good nature.

Still sitting at the feasting table, Kate observed the lively room and itched to retreat to her bedchamber, away from the crowd. She had told herself before she joined the festivities that she was only going to stay through dinner then retire. It was awkward being around so many people when she wore a lie, faking smiles to everyone around her as if she fared well. But she was far from well; she was barely hanging on. At times it was hard to breathe. All she wanted to do was unbraid her hair, take off her dress, and plunge back into bed.

Alice had done a beautiful job dressing her in a red long-sleeved dress. Kate had all but forgotten about the red Celtic scrolls wrapping around her arms when she had undressed in Alice's presence. Mortified that she had given her secret away, Kate hastily recovered her shift and hid the markings. However, Alice was forever keenly aware of her surroundings and had seen the knot-work. To Kate's relief she paid the markings no attention and handed Kate a beautiful red dress that covered her secret nicely. The woman had even worked her magic on her short hair. Starting from the front, Alice braided the brown strands back into sophisticated twists and weaves until all of her hair was tucked up neatly around her head. A perfect picture of a lady.

It was times like this when she didn't recognize the woman before her, without her normal black woolen tunic dress and the veil she'd worn all her life. The new attire was foreign.

Just as Kate had made up her mind that now was a good time to excuse herself, a man, tall and slender, approached her.

"Would ye like to dance?" the stranger asked with a vibrant smile.

Kate looked up at him and sat down nervously, brushing away an escaped strand of hair from her face. "Thank ye for asking, but mayhap another time."

The man eyed Kate, taking in her beauty. "Och," he said. "Ye be too bonny a lass to be sitting by yerself. May I sit?" The persistent man was not taking no for an answer. He seated himself across the table from her before she could speak.

"What's yer name?" he asked, taking a pull from his tankard.

"Kate."

"Well, I'm happy to meet ye, Kate. I'm Broc."

As Kate looked at him, she took notice that he was quite handsome. Blue eyes and blond short hair, one half of his face was flawless, on the other side a scar marred his left cheek. A warrior, she thought.

"'Tis nice to meet ye, Broc. If ye'd please excuse me—"

"I have no' seen ye around here. Ye be a friend of the laird's?"

Kate huffed. Broc wanted her company and he was going to have his way, whether she liked it or not. Oh, she could be rude and walk away. Truly that was what she felt like doing. But being rude was not in her nature.

"I am a friend of Lady Abigale."

The blond warrior took her hand and brought it to his lips. Quickly, Kate retracted her hand and held it to her chest. Wide-eyed, she sent him a ridiculing stare. How dare he make such a gesture? His lips most certainly did not belong on her skin. She stood, still glaring at the stranger. "I bid ye a good night."

Before Broc could open his mouth to proclaim how sorry he was for making her feel uncomfortable, Kate walked away. Grasping her chest, she tried to breathe through the thickened air in the hall. She shouldered her way through the crowd as she made her way to the door leading to the outside bailey, barely holding back the tears that threatened to fall. God's teeth, when was she going to reach the door?

With quickened strides, Kate shoved the double wooden doors open, welcoming the cool air into her seized lungs. She walked a few feet into the bailey and doubled over, taking in deep breaths. By the saints, she missed Hawk. She had made her best effort to hold it all together, yet she wasn't ready to let go. Everyone around her wanted her to cover up her wounded heart, but she wanted to let it bleed.

Kate looked up to the night sky, taking in deep breaths. "Hawk, why...why did ye have to leave me?"

From the corner of her eye a cloaked figure appeared, coming toward her from the far end of the bailey. She straightened her body as a shiver ran down her spine. She craned her head to get a better look at the stranger who was now approaching with long, determined strides. Her heart raced. Who was this cloaked person and what did they want from her?

Kate took a step back and thought about running to the great hall, but then the figure removed the hood of its cloak. Her eyes traveled down the blackened material, which revealed a brawny build hiding underneath. It had to be a man.

Kate followed her trail up and came to an abrupt stop. Her hands shook, tears collected at the corners of her eyes, her legs threatened to go weak. *It can no' be true.*

The hood fell to the man's shoulders and Kate gasped. Her quivering hands covered her mouth in disbelief as she met soft green eyes swirling intently. Trembling, Kate couldn't trust her eyes or herself. Was this one of her dreams? Closing her eyes, she shook her head, trying to erase the image before her, for her heart could not withstand any more pain if it was, in fact, a dream.

When she opened her eyes, the man stood, towering over her. His smoldering gaze heated her from the outside in. She didn't know what she was waiting for. If this was a delusion she didn't want it to go away. Perhaps he was real. *Just reach out and touch him, Kate.*

Reaching up, she hesitantly touched his lightly bearded jaw. "Hawk, she whispered. "'Tis ye?"

"Aye, lass, 'tis me."

Every bit of fear fell away. Tears of joy streamed down her face as she smiled up at him. Hawk cupped her face and thumbed away the tears.

Kate swallowed hard. "Ye're alive. I...I thought ye were..."

"Shhh, lass," Hawk whispered. "I be a dragon. No amount of fire can hurt me."

Kate leaned her head against his hand and closed her eyes, relishing his touch. She brought her hand up and placed it on his. "I never thought that I would feel ye again." She squeezed his hand. "Hawk, I know ye dinnae return my love. But I will never stop loving ye. Ye're in my soul."

Suddenly, big, strong hands clasped her shoulders and broke their embrace. When she opened her eyes, swirling depths stared straight into her with great force.

"Kate, I be a fool, a damn fool for letting ye go. I knew from the moment I met ye that ye'd be the one who broke through to me." Not waiting any longer, Hawk bent down and claimed her lips with a passion that rippled through her core. She grabbed the back of his head, bringing him even closer, deepening the kiss, kissing him thoroughly as if she couldn't get enough of his intoxicating taste.

He gripped her hips and pulled away as Kate continued to run her hands up and down his chest, fearing he would fade away.

"Kate, I love ye, lass."

For a moment Kate was speechless.

Taken aback, Hawk's brows furrowed. "What's wrong? Isn't that what ye wanted to hear?"

"I need more than words, Hawk."

"Kate, what do ye want from me?" he asked as he looked down at her.

She placed her hand over his heart. "I want yer heart."

Hawk shook his head. "I can no'—"

Placing her finger on his lips, she silenced him. She didn't want to hear any more excuses. He was going to listen to what she had to say. "I want ye to kiss me underneath a million bright stars until I can no' feel me toes. I want ye to touch me until me knees go weak. I want to know ye'll always be there for me." Kate looked down at her shaking hands that were still over Hawk's heart. "I want ye to love me, Hawk."

Her heart ached, for she knew if Hawk denied her now, it would be for good. She couldn't stand the heartache any longer. It was now or never.

Suddenly Hawk lifted her chin until they locked eyes. "Lass, ye had me heart the first time I saw ye. I was too damn stubborn to admit it."

Tears streamed down Kate's cheeks as she breathed in a shaky breath.

"Kate, I love ye and unfortunately ye be stuck with me because ye're never going to leave me sight again." He claimed her lips in a soul-crushing kiss that said more than any words ever could have. She cupped his face tenderly, caressing his cheeks with her thumbs.

Kate broke their kiss to take in a deep breath. "I knew it."

Hawk tucked a lock of brown hair behind Kate's ear. "Knew what?"

She smiled as she looked deep into his swirling eyes. "That ye had a heart."

Hawk grinned. He grabbed her hips and pulled her closer. "'Tis only because of ye. Ye broke down me walls, Kate. My heart is in yer hands."

"And I'll take verra good care of it, that I promise."

Hawk grabbed Kate's arse and lifted her up until she straddled him. She wrapped her arms around his neck and kissed him long and hard as he walked them toward the gatehouse tower.

The stairwell was dark, narrow, and wound up to the look-out. Every stride Hawk took he fought to keep his balance and not trip. By the stars and moon, the stairs seemed to go forever, one step after another. Perhaps if he could tear his lips away from Kate's, then the task wouldn't be so daunting. However, he missed her and grew impatient; he wanted to feel her body beneath him again.

With Kate giggling against his neck, Hawk kicked opened the door and slipped inside. With much regret, he placed her on her feet and shut the door. The room was small and not well lit.

Kate squinted, trying to take in the view when she turned and bumped into a wall of sinewy muscle. With lust-hooded eyes, she glanced up at Hawk. Without saying a word, he removed his cloak and laid it on the ground. One shoulder at a time, Kate slipped her arms from her dress, allowing it to fall and pool at her feet so she was naked before him. Hawk gently caressed her up and down her arms, marveling at her beauty.

Leaning her head back, Kate closed her eyes and melted beneath his touch. Her heart hitched when Hawk halted. "Ye have me markings?" She opened her eyes, stunned at his observation. Caught in the moment, she had all but forgotten about the light red swirls that decorated her skin.

Insecurely, she covered her marked skin with her hands. Hawk grabbed her wrists and kissed up her arms along the swirled marks. "Do ye understand what these mean?" he asked.

"I'm no' sure. They appeared after we had been together." Kate's cheeks flushed with the thought of the last time they had been alone together.

"My sweet Kate, this means ye be me mate." He looked at her with a grin.

Kate furrowed her brows. "Mate? What does that mean?"

A low primal growl escaped Hawk. "It means ye're mine, lass."

At that moment Hawk laid her down and made up for lost time. He pleasured her again and again, for he could never tire of this woman...his mate.

EPILOGUE

The ends of a red and gold ribbon rippled against the subtle wind. A babe in the distance softly cooed. A woman sniffed, holding back joyful tears. Words of undying love and happiness were prayed over them. And sweat slid down his temple as Hawk waited for the words he longed to hear. It wasn't that he needed the affirmation; he wanted to kiss his wife.

Hawk looked at the ribbon that joined their hands and forever bound them together. He gave a slight squeeze to her delicate hand, sending her comfort and encouragement as she placed the ring on his finger.

"I give this ring as a token of my undying love. For a ring has no beginning nor no end and symbolizes me love for ye." Her voice was soft and her deep hazel eyes held truth.

More words were said as the priest continued the ceremony, but Hawk paid them no attention. His sights were on the woman standing in front of him in red. Small embroidered gold dragons lined the ends of her long sleeves and continued on the sash she wore around her waist. But what amazed him the most were the red Celtic scrolls on her skin, peeking beneath the off-the-shoulder gown.

Kate cleared her throat. "Hawk," she whispered, "ye may now kiss the bride." She squeezed his hand in hopes of gaining his attention.

Shaking free from the spell he was under, he swallowed hard. He was so deeply enthralled with her beauty that he had completely blocked out everyone around him.

"Aye." He smiled and bent down, taking her lips, kissing her passionately. Wrapping his arms around her waist, he lifted her up and her arms flew around his neck. She smiled against his lips and Hawk knew right then and there that he would never love another like he loved Kate. "I love ye, Kate Comyn, Lady of Helmfirth."

The townsfolk of Helmfirth stood and shouted in celebration. Abigale sniffed back tears of joy while she bounced wee Jamie on her hip. The Dragonkine warriors in their best plaids and crisp clean tunics stood and walked over to Hawk, congratulating him.

Magnus and Fia approached their daughter and were warmly welcomed by a hug. Magnus kissed Kate on the cheek. "Lass, ye make a bonny bride."

Kate looked down at her dress, embarrassed by the compliment.

Fia stepped in and lifted her daughter's chin. "Kate, ye are bonny and there's no shame in it."

Kate smiled. "I was hoping that ye and Da would stay for a while. Perhaps we could become better acquainted? There are so many things I dinnae understand aboot me magic."

Fia smiled wearily at Magnus, waiting for his answer. There was still a lot of tension between them, but she hoped that Magnus would stay for their daughter's sake.

Magnus stood with his arms crossed over his chest; a pensive mood crept in. He cocked his brow and peered at Fia. "I think that would be a good start."

Kate beamed with joy and hugged her father tightly. "Thank ye, Da."

"Kate." Kate turned around and met her husband's eyes. "I have something I want to show ye."

Hawk took her hand and they excused themselves. They tracked through the glen on an open trail. Hawk stopped and pulled out a long black cloth, then folded it in half.

"What are ye doing, Hawk?" Kate asked, with a tinge of caution in her voice.

He approached his beautiful wife with the cloth in his hand. "Do ye trust me?"

"Aye."

"Good." Hawk wrapped the cloth around her head, covering her eyes. "Can ye see anything?"

"Are ye daft? Of course I can no'. Where are we going?"

"'Tis a surprise." Hawk took her hand and continued to lead her down the trail until they reached a small frame of a hut. He untied the blindfold.

Kate gasped. "Hawk, you rebuilt the mew." The roof was missing, but the walls were newly built. Kate remembered this area well; it was where Hawk kept his raptors.

"I have a gift for ye," he said. He whistled a distinctive tune and looked to the sky. Squinting against the brightness of the sun, Kate followed his gaze. A huge goshawk circled above them. Hawk extended his arm and the hawk swooped in and perched on his arm.

"This is Arlen, me goshawk."

"But I thought everything was destroyed," Kate said as she took in the hawk's beauty.

"Aye, I did too until I was out here rebuilding the mew, and Arlen was perched in that tree right over there." He pointed. "But there's more."

Kate smiled at her husband.

"Hold yer arm out like I have."

"Like this?"

Hawk nodded.

A white and brown merlin swooped down and landed on Kate's arm. The hawk fluffed its feathers and settled in.

"Och, Hawk, 'tis beautiful." Kate brought her hand up to stroke the raptor's head.

"She is beautiful and she's yours to train." He winked.

"I dinnae know what to say."

Hawk took the merlin and his goshawk and set them on a nearby branch. He turned to his wife and pulled her into an embrace. "Ye can start by saying ye love me, Kate Comyn." He nuzzled her neck.

She whispered in his ear. "I love you, Hawk, always."

About Victoria Zak

Victoria Zak is an internationally bestselling author of historical and contemporary romance. She weaves magic into her timeless tales, reminding readers anything is possible, especially with a dragon by your side. Raised in Dunedin, Florida, the sister city to Stirling, Scotland, no wonder she grew up fascinated with anything Scottish. Add the ocean into the mix, and it's easy to see where Victoria found inspiration for her stories.

As a child, she read anything she could get her hands on, which developed into full-scale book addiction by adulthood. Curious by nature, Victoria doesn't shy away from anything. She enjoys historical research and hanging out at the nearest coffee shop. Victoria currently resides in Maryland with her real-life heroes, her husband and two children.

Victoria loves to hear from her readers. You can connect with her through the links below:

www.victoriazakromance.com
victoria@victoriazakromance.com
Newsletter http://bit.ly/1uebjmR

 facebook.com/VictoriaZakAuthor

 bookbub.com/authors/victoria-zak

 instagram.com/victoriazakromance

 twitter.com/VictoriaZak2

BOOKS BY VICTORIA ZAK

Guardians of Scotland Series:

Highland Burn

Highland Storm

Highland Fate

Highland Destiny

Highland Hope

Ember Brooke Series:

Scorched Hearts

Hearts Under Fire

Daughters of Highland Darkness Series:

Beautiful Darkness

Deadly Darkness

Wicked Darkness

Hell's Cowboys Series:

My Immortal Cowboy

Stand Alones:

Once Upon a Winter Solstice

The Jewel of Grim Fortress

Midnight's Kiss

www.ingramcontent.com/pod-product-compliance
Lightning Source LLC
Chambersburg PA
CBHW032135170626
46808CB00006B/2246